Real Life

Books by Sharon Butala

Sharon Butala

Real Life

short stories

 Harper*Flamingo*Canada
A PHYLLIS BRUCE BOOK

Real Life: Short Stories
Copyright © 2002 by Sharon Butala.
All rights reserved. No part of this book may be
used or reproduced in any manner whatsoever
without prior written permission except in the case
of brief quotations embodied in reviews.
For information address
HarperCollins Publishers Ltd,
55 Avenue Road, Suite 2900,
Toronto, Ontario, Canada M5R 3L2

www.harpercanada.com

HarperCollins books may be purchased for
educational, business, or sales promotional use.
For information please write:
Special Markets Department,
HarperCollins Canada,
55 Avenue Road, Suite 2900,
Toronto, Ontario, Canada M5R 3L2

"Postmodernism" appeared in **Prairie Schooner**,
vol. 67, no. 4, winter 1993.
"Saskatchewan" appeared in a different form in
Canadian Fiction magazine, no. 80, 1992.
"Random Acts" first appeared as "Acts of Love" in
Story magazine, spring 1995; **The Penguin
Anthology of Stories by Canadian Women**,
Viking, 1997; and in **Due West: Thirty Great
Stories from Alberta, Saskatchewan, and
Manitoba**, Coteau Books, 1996.

First edition

Canadian Cataloguing in Publication Data

Butala, Sharon, 1940–
Real life : short stories

"A Phyllis Bruce book".
ISBN 0-00-255402-X

I. Title.

PS8553.U6967R42 2002   C813'.54
C2001-90252-1
PR9199.3.B798R42 2002

HC 9 8 7 6 5 4 3 2 1

Printed and bound in the United States
Set in Monotype Dante and Akzidenz Grotesk

In memory
of
Caroline Heath

Contents

Real Life

When I saw Dan enter the gallery where I was having a show, my knees went weak and I had to lean against the wall, casually, as if I were tiring of standing. In the unexpectedness of his appearance, a sudden memory engulfed me, more physical than anything—a kind of blooming of sensation around and in me, of smell and texture and colour—of how we had been together. It made my face feel hot, yet my fingertips against my wineglass shrank with cold.

When he spotted me, he approached, dodging people and sidling between them, and we stood, staring at each other, he with his hands thrust into the pockets of his raincoat, the shoulders spotted with rain, and me not knowing whether to smile or weep. The people I'd been talking to drifted away, one with a quick, speculative glance at me, the other carefully masking his expression before he turned away. I murmured, "Dan! Hello," in a breathy, pleased voice filled with surprise and, I suppose, my uncertainty. I held myself ready to brush his cheek with mine or maybe hug him, but he stopped too far away, and made no move to come closer.

"Edie," he said heavily, a name no one else calls me, so that even in my confusion I was touched with tenderness toward him. But he was looking around the small space packed with people sipping wine as if to find a quiet corner for us. "We can't talk here," he decided, firm, and his eyes shifted to a spot on the wall between paintings, briefly, while I waited, hardly breathing, hearing around us the tinkle of laughter rising above the steady buzz of voices. "I'll be at that café across the street at—say, eleven—tomorrow morning?"

He had been the most beautiful young man, on the small side, and with perfect, fine-boned features, as delicately fashioned as a woman's, but with a masculine quality, a combination I tried and tried to suggest in drawings and on canvas and never succeeded. Critics have labelled my work "passionate"; one had already referred to this show—nudes, all—as "brutal," which, to tell the truth, rather pleased me. Now I saw that the delicacy of line in Dan's face was blurred and thickened. All that booze, I thought, saddened, and then felt a twinge of nasty satisfaction and was immediately ashamed. It was a moment before I could get my mouth to shape a reply.

"All right," I said. "At eleven." My wineglass was suddenly too heavy to hold and I looked around futilely for a place to put it down. I turned back to him and saw that something, some intensity, had gone out of his eyes. They slid away from my face in an odd way, as if now he couldn't recall what he was doing here, and I wondered suddenly if he were ill—some terrible, life-threatening illness, I thought. But already he'd turned from me and was making his slow way out of the gallery. A few people, recognizing him, turned their heads to watch him go. He hadn't spoken again, and he hadn't looked at one of my paintings. I almost gave one of those quick snorts of mixed dismay, humiliation, and anger, but caught myself in time. I'd built up my women with a deliberate bruised raggedness, using a palette knife and dark colours to just hint at an undiscovered opulence, and now it seemed to me their eyes followed him, unblinking and filled with apprehension.

Dan and I had married when we were still students, me at the art school and Dan at the university on the other side of the city. We fell hard for each other, and we got married, because that's what you did then. Just a quick Justice of the Peace thing, telling no one, not even our parents. Dan had only an alcoholic father whom he blamed for his mother's too-early death, and I'd run away from home at sixteen. By that time I knew that I preferred any kind of life to the one I'd been raised in, and so I prepared myself, knew where I was going, what I would do to survive, took every precaution not to be found, including changing Edith-May to Raine (I used to love that glamorous *e* I'd put on the end), and adopting Hamilton, my grandmother's maiden name. Thinking back to that scared, determined teenager, I believe I chose a family name, knowing it was dangerous, because a tiny part of me was afraid to float completely free. I've never missed my father or my brothers, and my mother only once in a while—or maybe what I feel when I think of her is really longing for the mother I wish she'd been—but I have often missed the farm. More, in fact, now that I'm older—the colour and movement of the aspen forest behind the house, the sound of the wind whispering through the leaves, a certain smoky scent in the air that comes in the fall sometimes, even here in the city. Dan and I were married only a couple of years and, except for book covers or in the newspaper, I hadn't seen him in—it must be nearly thirty years.

I was sitting down across from him before he realized I'd arrived. I'd put a scarf over my short, unruly white hair—it's been white since I turned forty, a family curse, I like to say— put on dark glasses and, leaving my caftans, billowing pants, bracelets, and rings at home, wore dark cotton slacks and a sweatshirt under an old raincoat I'd found in the back of my closet. I was aware that this was some sort of statement, but I was too agitated to figure out what I was trying to say: *We have no secrets? You matter this little to me now?* As far as I could tell he was dressed no differently than he'd been the night before. I suddenly remembered that he'd liked clothes once, when he was young, nice sportscoats, trim slacks, he could take an hour to pick just the right shirt and tie. I'd loved that then, even if at the same time it had made me faintly uneasy. That he no longer cared about how he dressed didn't surprise me.

"On time?" he said, looking up. He didn't smile. "That's not like you." I thought, Is that all you remember about me? but I didn't say anything. He was sitting sideways to me, his still-skinny legs extended, one arm resting on the table. He nodded to the waitress; she came over and put a cup of coffee in front of me.

"Let's start again," I said, holding my voice steady. I took off my sunglasses, set them on the table, and gave him my best social smile. "It's been a long time. Congratulations on another book on the bestseller list. So nice of you to look me up."

"I didn't look you up," he told me, and gave a small, sour laugh. "I'm here to do a reading at the university. I'm at that hotel down the street—I walked past the gallery. I saw your name. On impulse, I went in."

"You *could* have gone on by," I said. When he didn't answer, the anxiety that had been building in me since the night before, that I thought I'd been containing pretty well, seeped out, and I said briskly, "What is it you want, then, if it isn't to go over fond memories?"

"You know it's been twenty-five years since Willie died." My mouth began unexpectedly to tremble—I should have known it would be about this—and I bent my head to hide it. What had I expected? I was asking myself, and had to fight down anger, mixed with something I recognized as self-pity. He expelled the air from his chest, then filled it again noisily.

"I—heard," I said, "as soon as it … happened." One crazed letter from John (whose real name was Vladimir, he was an escapee like me), blaming me for everything. Then years and years of silence, Dan—I'd read this in a magazine—struggling with alcoholism until his rehabilitation, maybe a dozen years ago now. "I'm very sorry." It came out a whisper and I cleared my throat.

"Do you know where John is?" he asked, for the first time turning his head to look directly at me. I was in control again, and spoke as casually as I could, as if it were nothing to me.

"He teaches history in Halifax, at some Catholic college." I saw then that he knew this and had merely wondered if I did. In the silence that followed I could not stop myself from remembering John shoving me away from him so hard that I hit a stud in the unfinished wall of my attic studio—he was six feet, and powerful, a farm boy from Alberta—my arms were bruised for weeks, the next day I could hardly move my back was so sore. He was sobbing when he did it. Maybe I was too, I can't remember. The strange thing was that although I knew I was hurt, at the moment of it happening, I felt nothing. I sometimes think of that—how I felt nothing. And other memories from my childhood—I took a deep breath through my nose and mentally shoved it all back into darkness.

"He had six children," Dan was saying. He laughed, but the sound was flat and unamused, painful to hear. "Katie and Joy"—these were John's two daughters with Willie—"and another four. He went to Ontario to teach—afterward. First, he smashed my windshield and tried to kick in my front door. Then he married again and went to Halifax—I bet she looks like Willie." For an instant Willie hovered between us, the gentleness she had, the way she would look at you with a kind of fond tenderness, like a mother at her grown-up child.

"Probably," I said, my voice as neutral as his. Then that sureness went out of his face as suddenly as it had last night, and I braced myself for some unbearable revelation, or an accusation.

"She's been haunting me," he said softly.

"What? You mean ... actual apparitions?"

He went on as if I hadn't spoken. "I think about her all the time. It's almost as bad as when she first died."

"So that's why you came last night."

"I told you it was an impulse."

"So why are we here, having this conversation?" I asked.

"Joy and Kate—they came to see me. Not very long ago." This stopped me, for an instant I couldn't speak, I hadn't thought of them in years.

"They came—why?" I asked, and had to clear my throat.

"They just wanted to know—what happened, I think." He said this as if he were talking about the neighbours or somebody he'd heard of once. I half expected him to yawn. It was bizarre.

"What did you tell them?"

"What could I tell them?" He'd been slouching in his chair and now he straightened, swivelled toward me, cupping his coffee mug in his palms, and staring into it instead of at me. "We fell in love. We left together. Their mother wouldn't leave without them, so they came, too. I knew it wasn't what they wanted to hear."

I made an "Mmmm" sound. But in the silence that followed another memory came welling up and I was immersed again in the ambience of the four of us in that house, John and Willie's, on a black and freezing winter night, snowbanks piled up around the walls and driveway and down each side of the town's streets, a high wind pelting the house with snow, whining around the windows and roof, giving all four of us an excuse for Dan and me to stay the night. Upstairs their two little girls asleep, and us in the living room, Willie woozy from wine, and the rest of us mellowed out, as we used to say, on pot. And that *something* drifting through the air. I remembered it still, I *felt* it; it came to me so clearly that the skin on my thighs prickled, and I shivered and pulled myself back to the shiny tabletop, the waitresses murmuring together across the room.

"After she died, their grief—John's sister came and got them, took them back to him. I went off the deep end there, for a while. No doubt you heard," he added, glancing at me. I nodded. "Then I couldn't get her out of my mind—I can't—I nearly started drinking again, I—" He stopped abruptly, as if shutting down that line of thought, and I had the urge to touch his hand in commiseration but resisted, as much because he had left me once, long ago, as because I knew he would pull away from my touch. I managed to keep my voice soft.

"How long has this been going on?"

"Months—I don't know. The girls—they're women now—really threw me." After a moment he said, "She was such a good person. She shouldn't have had such a terrible death."

"It doesn't help to sanctify her," I told him, resorting to briskness. There it was again, as if all these years hadn't passed at all. She was just pretty, she was just—sweet, while I—"She was pretty ordinary, actually," I said, testing him. I suddenly wondered if I'd said that before, when all of it was happening. Knowing me, probably.

"She wasn't ordinary," he said, although mildly, as if he couldn't be bothered to argue. "Or if she was, it was in a way that had nothing to do with why I loved her."

For an instant after Dan and Willie had left, I'd been stung, my pride was hurt, but then, I thought how I had John, that

John was mine now, and I saw that what had started out as a game, a distraction from that boring little city full of boring, provincial people, had turned into something else: it had turned into my deepest desire. I remembered that then I did not regret this in the least, and for the first time in a long time I knew I would cry if I let go, even a little.

"All these years have passed, nearly thirty years," I said. I didn't know what it was I wanted to say, I was struggling with something that refused to form itself into a question I could ask, or something I could say, like, maybe, *I suffered too, you don't know how bad it was.* "Hard to believe we once loved each other," I said finally, and I looked at him, afraid of what he might say, and yearning for his agreement in a naked way that shamed and puzzled me.

"We didn't love each other!" He sounded more surprised than angry. "We were just both so screwed up. We clung to each other like limpets cling to rocks. That's not love." I took my cigarettes and lighter out of my bag and, fumbling a little, lit up. I wanted to remind him of how good we'd been in bed, but I could see that he'd deny that too, and I knew that, even now, I'd do anything to avoid hearing that denial. I smiled carefully at him through my cigarette smoke.

"You're destroying my most cherished memories," I said. He spoke over my voice, abruptly, as if he could no longer hold it back.

"We killed her."

I wasn't sure, for an instant, that I'd heard him right. But then I knew I had, and I was suddenly very tired. So tired I could have put my head down on the table and gone to sleep.

"No," I said, as if I'd never, not once, thought of this myself. "Her decision to kill herself was hers alone."

I'd always wanted to paint her, nude, of course: she had a long-legged graceful body, her skin was pale and of the finest grain—but John would never allow such a thing. And I had no interest in doing the Madonna-with-children that he wanted, so I never painted her, or even drew her, not once. I would have questioned that beauty, I would have searched out the darkness in her—but Dan went on as if he hadn't heard my denial.

"John because he wouldn't leave her alone after she was gone, me because … I took her away, I put her in a position she wasn't strong enough to cope with, you because—"

"Because why."

"You started the whole thing." There was no accusation in Dan's voice, just a heaviness, as if he'd always known this and knew that I knew it, too. That we all did. That there was no point in histrionics any more, not even from me. "Willie and I would never have gotten together, she would never have—if you hadn't decided you wanted to sleep with her husband."

I wondered what would happen if I stood up and left. I imagined myself at home, pouring a stiff Scotch, turning on the television, letting Rosie, my cat, curl up on my lap. Nothing, I supposed. Nothing at all, but then I would never be finished with it, either.

"If it makes you feel any better, the moment you two left John dropped me," I said. "He never stopped loving his wife or wanting his marriage or his children. Maybe he was the only one who took it all in the right spirit." I paused, feeling heat rising in my face. "It was only supposed to be a diversion—" Then I said, "You were part of it too." I was becoming angry. "Nobody forced you. Or Willie."

Dan swung his head to gaze out the big plate-glass window through the ferns and various other potted plants, to the street where it had begun to rain harder. He shrugged, a barely perceptible acknowledgement of what I'd just said.

"And then we fell in love," he said and laughed briefly, quietly. "Joy seemed stunned and hurt and baffled all at once. Such a pale, shapeless little person she grew up to be. And Kate—" He shook his head. "Such hate, such rage. Maybe I deserve it." Funny how I hadn't thought of them, as if what happened to them, or how they felt about what had happened, belonged to a different universe than the one the four of us inhabited.

"Stop it," I said. "You can't change anything." Everything was coming back to me, all of it, and I hated him for finding me, hated myself for needing this meeting.

"You were ruthless," he said, "in those days. I always supposed it was that upbringing you had."

"I wanted what I wanted," I admitted, smiling faintly at him, as if his attacking me were nothing. I'd been cured of my ruthlessness, or at least I'd learned to look both ways, to consider, before I went after something.

"And you got off scot-free," he told me. "You're the only one of us who did." Now I had to turn my head away from him, as if I were just checking out the window to see if it was still raining or not. I'd stumbled after John, pulling at his clothes, falling as he jerked away from me; Dan hadn't seen me on my knees weeping when John was gone.

Years later, when I had a show in Halifax, I'd found John's address and written to him to say I needed to talk to him. I'd thought it best to prepare him, but he wrote back only, *Stay away from me!* I got up the courage on my next to last day there to phone him. I said, *John, talk to me, I'm afraid, I can't go on, I have to tell you*—and he hung up on me. My palms against my coffee mug were damp, as if the rain outside were spreading and all of us, sooner or later, would drown in it.

Dan and I were leaning across the restaurant table so that our heads were close together, each of us looking, not at each other, but at our reflections in its glossy plastic finish.

John and I had lain in each other's arms on the sofa, watching Willie mount the stairs with Dan as if she were drifting in a dream, as if none of what was happening were real. I suppose Dan believed he could make her real, make all of it real. I remember I'd closed John's eyes with my lips—in the lamplight and the night their blue-grey had deepened, it frightened me—I didn't dare let him watch his wife go up the stairs with another man. And I wanted him to remember that now he had me.

And what else had I wanted? Besides John? I wasn't sure I could remember. To shed my history, I suppose. To defy it, to pull myself free into some world where people didn't enslave you and call it love or duty or necessity, where beauty and even joy were possible.

While we'd been talking the lunch crowd had started to come into the café. If we didn't order lunch ourselves, we'd probably have to leave as more people gathered to wait for tables. I sat back then, knowing now I would never see Dan again.

"Who would ever have thought it would end this way," I murmured.

"What way has it ended?" Dan asked. "It hasn't ended."

The waitress arrived then and pointedly put our bill down on the table, neatly halfway between us. Dan reached into his pocket and threw a couple of coins onto the table. He pushed away the chair beside him with his foot, rose, and began to walk away. I followed, the crowd at the door moving aside to let us through.

Outside on the sidewalk we stood facing each other in the light patter of rain. The lunch-hour crowd parted and went around us, tilting their umbrellas away.

"I'm thinking of marrying again," he said. "A young woman—she thinks I'm a god," and he had the grace to laugh, although in a faintly sardonic way. "I don't want to be alone any more." He said this quietly, so I barely heard it. *This* was finally the reason he'd wanted to talk to me. For a moment, I couldn't speak.

"There is not much demand for old women," I said, my voice harsh.

The light at the end of the block changed and cars hissed by on the wet pavement, creating a cold wind that made Dan hunch and me pull up my collar. A woman hurried by, a spoke of her umbrella poking my head as she passed. She kept going.

"I wonder, is everyone's life like this?" Dan asked.

We looked at each other then, into each other's eyes, deeply, and in his, or in that moment, I saw what I had always known and denied. That this was real, had always been real, that long ago, the four of us, stranded in that snowy little city far from the capitals of the world, by doing what we did, met, or made, a fate that would keep us firmly tied to the earth until the gods took pity on us, and finally let us go.

Night Class

The memo from her department head asking her to teach the fall semester in one of the university's satellite programs lay on her desk. If she agreed, besides her regular teaching load, she'd be driving once a week to the monastery an hour from the city to fill in for Dr. Chomska, who'd had a heart attack. She saw the request at once as a chance to earn extra money and, Aaron uppermost in her mind, dismissed all her misgivings as quickly as they presented themselves: asking her mother to babysit yet again, the condition of her car, Chomska's course that she'd have to teach. She hesitated an instant, but then she was punching numbers on the phone and the department head's assistant was saying "Dr. Russell's office."

When she set down the phone, Christine found she was trembling: if it was with joy that she saw her fund for Aaron taking an unexpected leap, she was also, suddenly, picturing herself in the middle of the night stuck in a snowbank on a deserted country road. She might have changed her mind even then, but the phone rang, startling her out of her train of thought.

"Christine?"

"Yes," she said crisply, as if she were talking to a colleague or a workman she was thinking of hiring, instead of her husband who, as she told everyone, had abandoned his family and run off to Montreal as soon as the going got tough. She never said it, though, without experiencing a stab of guilt.

"I'm thinking about you and the kids." She imagined him seated at his desk in some chilly, grimly neat office, still wearing his bulky tweed overcoat, his mouth glum, his dark eyes magnified behind his thick glasses.

"Oh?" she said, mustering coldness, although far behind her eyes heat was rising that meant she might cry.

"Talk to me, Christine." She began to shove papers around on her desk.

"Things are fine," she told him. "Meagan has a cold, Mother is staying with her until she's better. Aaron …" She hesitated.

"Aaron is as usual?"

Involuntarily she placed her fingertips on her chest, over her heart. She said, "Yes, the same." He started to speak, but she spoke over his voice, hurried, her own strained and too high-pitched. "I found—there's a new program—it's there, in Montreal—"

"Public or private?"

"Private, but really—"

He made an exasperated sound. "It's hopeless, Christine."

She pulled the phone away from her ear, almost dropped it into its cradle, but at the last instant held back. "I'm determined to try this, Graeme." She paused. "Last hope," she said, she could give him this much, and made a sound meant to be a laugh. "I'm teaching a night class to help pay for it. I'm writing to ask for government funding; I'm going to write to that big telethon. I'm not going to give up until—"

"Until what?" Graeme asked. "Until your mother's dead from the stress? Until Meagan is destroyed? Until there's no one left but you and Aaron, and not even Aaron because he doesn't know where the hell he is—"

She dropped the phone into its cradle and stood, blinking, her hands pressed against the heat in her cheeks. Immediately the phone rang again and she picked it up without quite realizing she had.

"I'm sorry," Graeme said.

"There's nothing left to say. We've said everything."

"I'm waiting for you to get it, Chris," he said quietly. "It isn't that I don't love you. You know I only went this far away because this was the only job I could get."

"Two years," she said.

"Not quite eighteen months," he answered her, and laughed softly, whether at her, their situation, or something she didn't know about, she couldn't tell. He must have a woman, she thought. Of course he has a woman. There was another long silence, but it seemed to her it buzzed with all the arguments, all the things each of them had said over and over again, and her palm grew damp against the plastic of the phone.

"I *will* come back," he said then. "If …"

"If I give my child away, if I hand him over to some institution, just pretend he never happened."

"More or less," Graeme said. His voice was flat, and she noted defiantly that he no longer bothered to qualify this or argue with her. "I can't wait forever," he said. Another silence, while she pressed her hand against the grimace she could feel beginning to distend her mouth.

"I have to go now, I'm due in class. I'm sending money," he said and hung up the phone so quietly that she was for a second not sure he had.

The road to the monastery was a narrow secondary highway that wound between grass-covered, yellow hills and past copses of trees radiant in their fall golds and oranges. It was early evening and the shadows were long, the golden light of late day turning the dull countryside into a strange, unearthly kingdom. She hadn't done any country driving in a long time, and she found herself slowing so that she could enjoy the landscape which she found unexpectedly lovely. Maybe in the coming summer she could find a way to take the children to a lake for a week or two. They were growing up without ever seeing nature, she thought, and it was as if a whole new dimension of life entered her thinking for the first time in a long time, and she wondered if this meant that finally she was getting over Graeme.

For a moment, she even forgot the long winter ahead of her of travelling by herself down this road. In this gentle beauty it was hard to worry about winter. And there was Chomska's course that she'd agreed to teach: Introduction to Postmodernist Literary Theory. A ton of work, texts to read she'd so far mostly managed to avoid, she'd found them so objectionable. She who had been raised on books, the pure, sumptuous world they opened for her, the passion. "It's this course or nothing," her department head had told her in his fake-jolly manner, when she'd timidly suggested they change it to one she was used to teaching. As if he didn't know that despite her relative youth—she was twenty years younger than Chomska—she was the last old-fashioned humanist in the English department.

At its outskirts she turned down a gravel road that skirted the town. Far ahead of her a small forest stood, orange and gold against the sea of dusky summerfallow surrounding it. The tall white spire of a church she'd been told to look for rose above the trees on the far side. Her car's small tires crunched and slid, and she slowed, not used to driving on gravel.

The monastery itself was much larger than she'd imagined, built of faded red brick, crumbling and patched-looking, with obvious newer additions on one end. The park surrounding it was bigger, too, than she'd thought when she'd seen it from a mile or so away, and through the trees to one side she could make out a neat row of smaller frame buildings. Her nervousness rising, she parked, pulled her briefcase out of the back seat, and crossed the parking lot to the wooden double doors.

A monk stood just inside them, evidently waiting for her. He held back the heavy door for her and introduced himself as the abbot.

"It's good you arrived a little early," he said. "I always show the new faculty around the first evening, answer questions, that sort of thing." He was perhaps sixty, a little stout in his worn black cassock, going bald, and so close-shaven that his face shone with a pink light.

"Thank you ..." She couldn't think how to address him and bowed her head to hide her confusion.

"Call me Dominique," he told her, "or Father Dominique."

He led her down long corridors with either polished and echoing wooden floors or worn vinyl tiles, opening doors as he went to show her classrooms, the cavernous, gleaming-clean kitchen, and the stark guest rooms.

"Sometimes faculty uses them when a winter storm blows in unexpectedly," he told her. They turned this way and that, climbed stairs and descended others, until she was lost. At one point he'd gestured toward a narrower hall to their left, it seemed to her less brightly lit than the others, and said that it led to the monks' residence and that it was, of course, off-limits to everyone else. Then he hurried her on.

"This is our library," he said, and stood back to allow her to cross the threshold into a long, high-ceilinged room full of rows of book-laden shelves. A half-dozen stern-looking old men in plain, dark-wood frames frowned down on the few students, all young and male, lost in study at the oak tables which ran in a long column down the room's centre. She smiled at the abbot, nodding politely, although the pictures offended her and the smell in the room of old floor wax or of oiled wood was distasteful.

"I'll show you our chapel and then you'll have had the inside tour. We run a full-scale farm here too, and we have an orchard and a very large vegetable garden, plus cows and laying hens." He turned to her now, and smiled down at her in a friendly, easy way that suddenly, frighteningly, made her want to nestle her head against his plump chest. "We're pretty much self-sufficient here."

"No women," she pointed out before she could stop herself. She hoped she'd said it in a joking tone, but she could hear her voice hanging in the air, forlorn, like a minor note on a piano.

"No, no women," he agreed amiably. "But many women come here for spiritual retreats or to attend programs. We aren't like those monks on Athos who don't even allow females on the premises."

The chapel was even larger than the library, and in contrast, very modern, with sleek pews of polished blond wood, white walls, and a stylized, terra-cotta crucified Christ on the altar. It was empty, but in their moment's halt so she could look around, Christine became aware of a sound invading the chapel's intense quiet, a deep-voiced, rhythmic murmur. The abbot was glancing about as if to check if anything was out of place or needed fixing. Beside him, Christine stood motionless, listening.

Male voices were filtering through the unbroken wall behind the altar, and though the sound was muffled, rising and falling, sometimes fading out to return on a louder note, it gradually came to her that it was chanting.

"It is our monks at evening prayer," the abbot murmured, oddly formal now.

She found herself advancing a few steps toward the sound, her head cocked. It's like the beating of a human heart, she thought, full of wonder, it's as if it is my own heart beating, and heat rose into her cheeks, she felt a quivering start in her abdomen and solar plexus and wondered, Am I ill? What is this?

Father Dominique turned briskly to her.

"I'm sure you want to do a little preparation before your class arrives." Obediently, Christine followed the purposeful swish of his skirts out of the chapel.

Night had fallen when she began her solitary drive back to the city. The road was deserted; no other headlights disturbed the darkness and no stars were visible; only the rare yardlight on a farm miles back from the road lit a small orange triangle in the sea of black. Christine was exhausted, leaning back in her seat as she drove, her head against the cushioned backrest. The class had gone well, she thought, although only one of her twelve students was a man—strangely, much older than the others, older even than her by at least fifteen years—and extra attentive, not in a studently way, she thought, but rather as if he found her an interesting phenomenon that would bear watching. She smiled nervously in the darkness as she thought of him and the way he held his mouth, sympathetically she found, and for no reason she could pinpoint, she was assailed by the penetrating sadness that nowadays seemed to be always present beneath whatever lightheartedness she might briefly find. Or had it always been this way? Surely in childhood she'd often been purely happy? But she wasn't sure.

Her mind circled around and came back, as it always did, to seven-year-old Aaron. Was he happy? she wondered. He did something that might be called play: he walked in circles, he rocked until she stopped him, he banged his head sometimes, although that behaviour was almost eradicated. He would sometimes sit on her knee while she read a story to Meagan, but then he would hum tunelessly, more a drone really, and usually it would escalate to that high, purposeless, meaningless scream of his, and nothing she said or did would stop it. She thought of his tense little body perched restlessly on her lap. Never an instant of relaxation until he fell asleep, never anything that might be called cuddling. Tears sprang to her eyes, but she refused them relentlessly. Crying had not so far cured him; she doubted it would do so now and sat forward in the seat, grasped the steering wheel more firmly, and accelerated the sooner to escape this darkness through which she drove.

When she pulled up in front of her house she'd already seen that all the lights downstairs were on, although it was nearly eleven. She stopped with a jerk, grabbed her briefcase, and rushed up the sidewalk and into the house. Her mother was waiting in the hall, her face white, her arms in their unravelling green wool sweater hugging herself tightly.

"It's okay, Christine, it's okay now," her mother said before she could ask. "He's back in bed. He's asleep."

For a long second Christine could only stare, her heart was in her throat, choking off her voice. She slumped against the wall, her briefcase falling to the floor.

"What happened?"

Her mother was smaller even than Christine and thinner, too, a tiny woman, really, gazing up at her out of large, steady brown eyes, whose colour tonight had darkened to black.

"I left his door unlocked when I put him to bed. Meagan called me and I went to her—I forgot the door wasn't locked—and ..."

"I forgot to lock the front door when I went out?" Christine asked and, without waiting for an answer, moaned, "How could I be so stupid?" Her mother shrugged, "Or I did. I think it was me." Christine straightened, began to shrug out of her coat.

"Was he gone long? Where was he? Who found him?"

"About forty minutes. The police." Her mother was helping her take off her coat, moving aside the briefcase. "He was running down the centre of Fourteenth, shrieking and flapping his arms, the way he does. Perfectly happy to go with the policeman."

"God," Christine said.

"Indeed." This was tart. "I'm thinking it's time you—"

"Mother"—a warning. Her mother turned, walked toward the kitchen. "I need a drink, Mom."

"Go check Meagan, and I'll mix you one."

The key to Aaron's room was, as always, hanging on the doorknob. She turned it softly in the lock and pushed open the door. He lay on his stomach, his face turned toward her, the wedge of light from the hall showing her his long dark eyelashes, his sweetly curved mouth, the mass of curly dark hair. He'd pushed aside his quilt and his pyjamas were twisted on his defenceless little calves.

She came forward, deciding against trying to straighten his pyjamas for fear of waking him, pulled the quilt gently up over him, and touched his curls softly, the familiar anguish welling up in her chest. She pushed it down, blinking, then went softly out, turning the key in the lock, letting it drop to hang on its cord from the handle. She never did this without a mix of satisfaction, that he was safe and would remain so until morning, and of guilt, that she, a mother, was her child's jailer.

Meagan lay primly in her bed, her five-year-old body hardly disturbing her blankets, one smooth, plump hand with its chipped green nail polish on three fingers resting neatly on the quilt, her barrette still holding back her straight fine brown hair that was exactly like Christine's. Christine bent and kissed her cheek, then carefully unclipped the barrette and slipped it out.

The street lamp beside the house cast a bar of light across the foot of Meagan's bed, turning the pink-flowered quilt a ghastly blue-mauve. Staring down at it, Christine was reminded of the long drive back through the moonless night, the purr of the motor, and then the pulsing of the monks' voices came back to her: the richness of the sound, and its rhythms, as if the monks were calling to lure some unseen, unknown, but precious thing.

In the living room her mother had already set out two of Christine's wedding-present, cut-glass tumblers on the coffee table and was pouring a little Scotch into each one. Christine fell into the armchair across from the sofa. Her mother began, "He's already in daycare, what difference …" Christine moved angrily, crossing her legs and then uncrossing them.

"We need to talk," her mother said after a moment, adding ice, not looking at Christine.

"Does it have to be now?" She reached to take the drink.

"Yes, now," her mother said, sitting down on the sofa.

"I'm not ready for the institutional route yet," Christine said stubbornly. "You know I'm not. Besides, there's still that clinic in Montreal—"

"Nobody's going to pay for that and you know it," her mother said. "I just want to tell you to call that special service for a sitter next Wednesday. I have a doctor's appointment." Christine nodded, leaned back, and closed her eyes briefly. "You can forget Graeme. If he wanted to help, he'd never have left in the first place. He'd send the money on time, he'd—" Christine raised both hands to her face, forgetting she was holding a glass, spilling her drink. "I'm sorry," her mother said. Christine put her hands down, blinking, setting her drink on the table beside her chair, brushing with the other hand at the beads of liquid quivering on the smooth navy fabric of her skirt.

"I can't let you go on this way, Chris. It's too hard to watch you struggling to keep up with everything. Aaron taking every drop of energy you have. Meagan not getting the attention she needs—"

"Mom …" Christine began.

"As if it's your fault the way Aaron is," her mother said. "You always were hard on yourself." Tenderness had crept into her voice. She sighed, and when she spoke again, her voice was wry, Christine could hear her struggling against her anger. "One day soon you're going to have to give it up."

She meant Christine would have to give up the fight to keep Aaron with her, which surely, at bottom, was based on the stubborn belief, no matter what her common sense and all the experts said, that one day he'd wake up and say, "Good morning, Mother, I'd like toast for breakfast," and everything would be fine at last.

"If I don't love him," she said, "no one will. You know that's true, Mom." Her mother opened her mouth as if to speak, then closed it again. This, too, was familiar to Christine. She could read her mother's mind: *But he doesn't know the difference.*

The next week the air had a crisp bite to it, the brilliantly coloured leaves had fallen and been blown away, leaving behind the forked black branches of trees stretching harshly against a sky resonant with light. Still, the very clarity of the light, the pale fields she caught glimpses of stretched out between the ranges of hills, and the flocks of crows and black-birds that swept away in unison at the approach of her car pleased and soothed her. How Meagan would love the birds, she told herself, imagining her delight in them as they lifted and swirled away.

More relaxed this week, at break she followed her students to the gloomy, dark-wood-panelled dining room with its long rows of tables and chairs where the monks provided coffee and cookies. As she stood in the coffee lineup, the only male in her class, Richard, came toward her from the urns, carrying two full mugs.

"You shouldn't spend half your break waiting in line," he said to her as he handed her one of them. Touched, she accepted it, feeling her face flush, then turned and sat down at the nearest unoccupied table. He followed, sitting across from her, reaching for a paper napkin from the dispenser and stirring two sugar cubes noisily into his mug. He was short and heavily muscled and wore his grey-blond hair in a long ponytail down his back.

"Are you married?" This startled her, but glancing at him she saw that this was not a pass, although what it was, she couldn't tell.

"Separated. You?"

"Long divorced, no children, considering whether I should become a Bride of Christ or not." He grinned at her. She was confused, and asked him, "Why did you ask me that? What do you mean—a Bride of Christ?" He didn't take his eyes from her face and she felt his gaze as too intimate, although not in the sexual way she found herself craving. She lowered her eyes to her coffee.

"You look tired. I bet you have children."

"Yes," she said. "Two." The rest of the class were pulling out chairs and sitting down around them.

"I meant that I'm considering joining the order here as a brother." Surprised again, she studied his face. It was lined, he must be fifty, she thought, and it seemed to her there was a darkness or uncertainty lurking in the backs of his eyes, despite his composed, even peaceful expression, which now appeared less than sincere to her. She stirred her coffee.

"Then you're not an English major. Why are you taking my class?"

"You were short the minimum twelve students. Father Dominique called me and I thought it might be interesting."

"And is it?" she asked him. Hearing the inadvertent huskiness in her voice she cleared her throat carefully, as if to explain to him that the coquettish sound had been a mistake.

"Too soon to tell," he said, grinning easily.

"Why do you want to become a monk?" she asked, then twisted her napkin in embarrassment at her own question.

"Oh," he said. "You mean, why would men choose to live without women?"

"No!" she said, taken aback. "It was a stupid question. I'm sorry." Smiling, he moved his hand, dismissing her apology.

"One doesn't choose to live without this or that, so much as one chooses to live with ..." He stopped and she wanted to ask him, "With what?" but what she found coming into her mind was an image of Graeme in bed with her, his smooth scholar's hand moving down her naked torso, and before she could stop it, desire was flooding through her.

"I have to get my notes organized," she said abruptly, and rising, set her mug by the urn, and went hurriedly out.

But once outside in the long, empty hall, she found she wasn't sure which direction to go to get back to her classroom. Tentatively, she moved forward. The first three doors along this hall were closed, she was sure she'd left her classroom door open, and besides, now she noticed there were no lights on in any of the rooms. Puzzled, uncertain whether to keep on this route or to turn back and try another, she hesitated. Up ahead was a dead end and another hall running perpendicular to this one, and now that she thought about it, she was sure they'd turned at least once on their way here. Encouraged, she walked quickly forward and at the corner, turned left.

But this couldn't be it: This hall was not as brightly lit, and there was something, some ambience, she wasn't sure what it was, that was subtly different from the hall she'd just come through. She paused uncertainly, lifting her head like a deer sniffing the air for danger, trying to assess what this strange, but compelling quality was. Some—stillness—for lack of a better word, an intense quiet that was not so much a mere lack of palpable sound, but an *attendance,* as if the molecules of air that hung invisibly around her held both patience and intent. It seemed to her, in her moment's halt, that this was what, without even recognizing it was so, she'd been for years now, longing. Something to fill Graeme's absence—no, more, something to fill the hollow left by her father's death, by all the nameless and unremembered childhood hurts, to replace the anguish that was Aaron, by the grappling with daily life. She held herself still, not breathing, and waited.

A door ahead of her opened and a monk—no, it was Father Dominique—backed out of a room, murmuring softly to someone inside. He turned and strode away from her down the hall, his robe making the air whisper, his feet drawing an authoritative squeak from the wooden floors. Christine realized that she'd strayed into the monks' quarters. In the instant it took for this fact to sink in, just before she turned and hurried away in the direction from which she'd come, she found herself straining to hear the sound of chanting, wanting with every cell to stay until she found the room where the monks lost themselves in their age-old prayer.

In mid-November Meagan came down with measles and had to stay home for a week. Her mother moved in with them to care for her, and then for Aaron when he arrived home from his special-needs daycare. Mid-semester was always a time of steady, droning work: seeing students, preparing lectures, teaching, doing her research and preparation for her night class, or attending meetings. Taking time off because a child had measles bordered on the impossible. And Aaron was sure to come down with it next. Ill, he seemed stricken by a kind of frenzy that made him even more unmanageable, as if the new sensations in his body terrified him, or threw him so off balance that what little control he had was destroyed. Sure enough, a few days after Meagan's diagnosis, Aaron developed the telltale spots too.

By the end of the week her mother was looking drawn, her dark eyes sunken, as if she were carrying on by sheer will alone. After Christine's father's early death and the worst of the grieving, her mother, with the strength of which Christine was still in awe, had squared her jaw and carried on raising Christine and her two brothers on her own. Now all of this vigour seemed drained from her, and although Christine said nothing—her mother was nearly seventy, after all—she watched her when her mother wasn't looking, urged her to bed early, while she bathed the children herself and got them into their beds. No matter what, she told herself grimly, measles don't last forever.

Christine was standing at the door putting on her coat when, behind her on the red-painted chest, a remnant from the blissful first days of her marriage when it seemed only the gayest colours would do, the phone rang.

"It's Graeme," her mother said. Christine glanced out to where her car sat in a fog of exhaust, warming up for her drive to the monastery. Reluctantly, she took the phone.

"I've decided to come back at Christmas for a few days to see the kids." Christine waited. "I thought maybe I'd take Meagan for a week, go out to the coast and see Mother and Dad."

"I guess that would be okay," Christine said. That he would not take Aaron was hardly a surprise.

"If you would arrange for Aaron to go into that home—just for the week—you could come with us." When she didn't reply, he said, "Chris?" In the brief silence she'd seen the three of them on the plane, Vancouver in all its damp beauty and calm, and then Aaron banging his head rhythmically against the floor or wall as he sometimes did, and no one holding him gently before he hurt himself. They would give him tranquillizers, they would tie him in his chair or bed. Would they strike him?

"I'm going to be late for class," she told him. "Mother will fill you in." Her mother took the receiver. She was saying, "They both have measles," as Christine shut the door behind her.

She drove through the city, down streets covered with snow tinted purple by the powerful street lights, past the university, its stone buildings shadowed and unwelcoming now, onto the highway, and then onto the narrower, darker road that led to the abbey. It always shook her to talk with Graeme. She wanted to hate him, sometimes succeeded, but never for long. And even when she hated him, the truth was she still persisted in loving him. Surely it was only because there was no one else in her life to help her erase his hold on her? She missed him, sometimes terribly, she missed his body against hers in bed.

A spasm passed through her gut, a clenching inside her, so that she bent over the steering wheel, making a strangled noise that sounded like a sob. She hadn't known the depth of her own need, and the need itself, and the fact of her not even knowing, frightened her so badly that for an instant the void of her own insanity opened before her, and she cast about frantically for something calming to grasp onto.

The monks came to her then, the quiet way they walked, the

mild way they spoke to her as she passed them in the hall or sat near one of them at coffee break. In what peace they must live, she thought, that *attentiveness* in the air around them—and her body tensed, listening for the deep throbbing of their voices in prayer. What was it they said? she wondered. *Help me*, maybe? Or *Succour—Give me succour?*

Richard was late to class.

"Sorry, Christine," he mumbled as he made his way to his seat. "I was talking to the abbot and just forgot the time." She'd come to her lecture on counter-arguments to the theories she'd been teaching, and when Richard was settled, she asked the class for any flaws they might have spotted themselves.

Richard said, "Aren't postmodernist critics saying there is no art? As well as no authority? How are we to go on if this is true?"

"You just hate the new stance because you're a middle-aged white man," a young woman answered him. "And it takes away your built-in authority—" Richard moved his head in irritation.

"How powerful do I look to you?" he asked, and without waiting for an answer, went on, his voice growing in force. "I reject it because it would destroy the known world and offer nothing in its place. It would have us slide back into anarchy."

Christine found herself thinking of Aaron running down the street in the night, flapping his arms as if he were a bird or plane, screaming in that mindless, high-pitched, piercing way of his, that nothing would stop, that had finally caused Graeme to rush out the door, before—Christine saw it, she remembered it now, suddenly, with horror, how could she have forgotten?—before he caught his own small son up in his arms and strangled him.

•   •   •

The last trip before Christmas. Christine pushed aside a stack of student essays and set the phone down solidly in front of her.

"Mom?"

"What's up, Chrissie?" her mother asked, and the note of weariness in her voice struck Christine to the heart, so that for an instant she couldn't remember why she was calling.

"Not much," she said, "I mean—I have to ask a favour of you." Her mother said nothing. Christine knew this to be her cue to back off, but her elbow rested against a pile of unmarked exams, and another pile sat on the shelf. "Can you look after the kids after school until I get back from the country?" For a moment her mother was silent, and Christine had a feeling she was holding back something she wanted to say, but she pushed this intuition aside in the face of the extremity of her need.

"I suppose I could."

"I'd never ask you, Mom, but I've stacks of papers to mark and I can't miss the faculty meeting at four, and I leave for the abbey at six-thirty and I just don't see how I can get home."

"I know, I know," her mother said. "Christine, I'm warning you"—Christine's heart gave a thump—"that this can't go on. Something's got to give."

"I know it, Mom," Christine assured her. "If we can just get through this week. Then I'm off for almost three weeks and we can both get a rest."

"Right," her mother said. "I'll get Meagan from kindergarten and I'll be there when the bus drops Aaron off." Then she hung up. For a long moment Christine sat at her desk with her elbows resting on it, her head in both hands.

There was to be a Christmas gathering of the faculty in the foyer after the meeting, and Christine had hoped to be able to attend for a while. She so rarely got out, never saw men socially it seemed to her, and what hope was there of another relationship if she never met anyone? Besides, she'd heard Peter Wilmer in Communications was divorcing. She'd once sat on a committee with him, and had been attracted to his boyish face and his easy manner. She thought hopefully that if they had a chance to talk casually at a party, they might hit it off.

But the meeting dragged on and she had to leave before it ended. She squeezed her way out of the row and made her way as silently as she could up the wide steps to the doors at the back. In the cloakroom she found her thick jacket, scarf, and mitts, picked up her briefcase which bulged with her night class's exams, and made her way regretfully out of the otherwise empty building into the crisp winter evening outside.

It must have been snowing during the meeting. While the car warmed, she brushed a thick layer of the light, sparkling stuff off the windows and the hood. Glancing upward anxiously, she saw that although it hadn't cleared yet, the sky had lifted and it looked as if the snowfall had ended. Encouraged, she got in, drove off the campus and out onto the street, where the fresh layer of snow lifted around her tires in a thin, glittering cloud as she passed. It made her think of walks with Graeme on nights like this, before the children were born. How they'd stood under the trees by the night-black river watching the snow fall, and embraced and kissed, their faces cold and wet with snowflakes, while inside their bodies heated, aching to meld together. Then she had thought they would go on forever in just that way.

About ten miles out of the city it began again to snow lightly. At the twenty-mile mark the fall was thicker. The air must have grown colder too, because the flakes that were falling were small and dry and hit the windshield with a shower of faint pings. Snow was beginning to cover the road ahead of her, so that when she passed rapidly through the inches-deep fall, it rose high around the car and, for an instant, obscured the road. She would have driven more slowly, but she was afraid she'd be late. Often, though, she had no choice but to brake until she could see again.

At thirty miles the wind had risen, blowing the snow across the road in perpendicular sheets so that she gripped the wheel hard and leaned forward to peer out the windshield in an effort to keep right of the centre line which disappeared in the blowing snow, reappeared, and then vanished again. She began to be afraid. The intervals when she couldn't make out the yellow line were lasting longer and longer; she was slowed to half her usual speed, and now she just hoped to stay on the road.

Sheets of snow swept across the hood, hitting the glass, and whirled away into the darkness. It seemed she'd driven straight into the heart of a storm, for suddenly the wind was stronger, the air much colder, and the heater was barely keeping the windshield clear of frost. As she peered ahead, the road vanished completely in the dizzying whirl of snow blowing in an unbroken, rolling screen across the hood. She flicked on her headlights to high to see if visibility would be any better, but she could see only a howling wall of white. She braked, dropping her hands from the steering wheel and slumping back in her seat. Terror nipped at her—this was just what she had most feared when she took this night job—and she fought to keep it away.

Abruptly, a break appeared in the wall of white pommelling the car; she could see ahead for perhaps thirty feet. She took her foot off the brake and the car rolled ahead again, picking up speed. Then, as suddenly as the storm had opened, it closed. She braked hard, the car fishtailed on the loose snow and the ice that had formed beneath it, skidded sideways, hit a bank of drifted snow along the shoulder, ploughed through it, and she was in the ditch and, Christine guessed, on the wrong side of the road.

She sat trying to slow her mind down enough to assess her situation. Then she edged the door open a crack and saw that the wind was sweeping the snow past so fast that the ditch wasn't filling. At least she wouldn't be suffocated. That grim task done, she checked the gas gauge—nearly full. She'd filled the tank on the way to work this morning. She put both hands against her cold cheeks, trying to think. What else was there? Oh, yes. She put the car back in gear and eased the gas pedal down to see if she could crawl back onto the road. But no, she needed new tires, these hadn't sufficient grip. Or she needed somebody behind pushing.

Surely the storm would blow itself out in a couple of hours, and what about the Mounties—they were always out checking the highways for people in trouble during blizzards. Someone would find her, she felt sure. There was nothing to worry about, she muttered to herself. In the meantime, she would get the sleeping bag and, using it to keep herself warm, wait for her rescuers. With difficulty she crawled backward between the seats, but the kit wasn't in the back seat, and when she looked further back under the hatch, it wasn't there either.

She knew where it was: sitting in her office. She'd had to borrow a heavier sleeping bag from one of her friends at work; she'd bought candles in the bookstore and a chocolate bar in the cafeteria. They were all together where she'd left them when she'd hurried out to the meeting, in a bundle behind her desk. She remembered how harrassed she'd felt as she'd closed the door, how something nagged at her that she couldn't iden-tify, how something was always nagging at her that she'd only partly done, or not done at all.

She sat with her mittened hands still uselessly clutching the steering wheel, too afraid to think, while a driving wall of white came at the car, seeming from all directions at once, striking it with such force that it felt as if at any moment she might be whirled away and lifted clear of the earth.

Shivering in the cab of the monastery's ton truck which was used, Father Dominique told her, to haul vegetables to the farmer's market in the summer, her car being towed behind, he explained that when the weather had turned bad he'd called her home to find she'd already left, and that there'd been no answer to his call to the university.

"So, when you didn't arrive on time, I set out to look for you." From the cab's added height she could see the road reasonably well even though the storm hadn't abated, and she saw now that if she'd had a bigger vehicle, she'd probably have been all right. She wondered if her mother or one of her brothers would lend her the money to buy a better car. She saw that this was a sensible thought, one she should have had sooner, and caught a glimpse, suddenly, amazingly, into her own recalcitrance, how she failed, wilfully, to grasp the truth of her life.

"We've cancelled classes," Father Dominique said, and she turned her head slowly toward him. "Too dangerous for students coming in from the country. You'll have to stay the night. And your husband has called a couple of times. He wants you to phone him when you arrive." Christine wondered what could be so important it couldn't wait until she got home. Her mother could take care of any emergency, Graeme knew that, so it had to be something other than the children. Maybe his father had died? He'd been ill. But Father Dominique was pulling up at the monastery doors, as if they'd just been out for a pleasant evening drive. "You go get warm. Brother Gerald will take you to your room. I'll look after your car."

Wearily, she climbed down from the truck. Wind-driven

snow whipped her hair and stung her face as she struggled to open the heavy door. A monk she hadn't seen before came toward her as she stood inside stamping the snow off her boots. He was short and thin and at least seventy, with sparse grey hair on a head that trembled faintly as he spoke to her. He led her to an office, unlocked the door, switched on the light, indicated the phone on the desk, and handed her the slip with Graeme's number on it. She was a little taken aback by the abruptness of all this, having had time only to step out of her boots and slip her icy feet into her shoes. But now, not even bothering to take off her jacket, she dialled the number he'd given her. Graeme answered before the phone had finished its first ring.

"Christine?" Suddenly, she saw Aaron dead on the road, a car speeding away; she saw her house engulfed in flames.

"What? What is it?"

"You better sit down." Her heart pounding, her mouth dry, she dropped into the chair behind the desk.

"Your mother's had a heart attack. She's in the university hospital. The kids—"

"The kids?"

"They're fine. She's quite a woman, that mother of yours. When she started to feel herself getting sick, she phoned that sitter you use sometimes, and then, while she was waiting for her to arrive, and she felt herself getting worse, she phoned me so that I could find you. And then she called 911 to tell them she was having a heart attack." He laughed briefly.

"Is she—all right?" Although she must be, or surely he wouldn't be talking to her in this half-jovial way.

"Well, she's not fine, but she's stable and she's in good hands." He gave her the doctor's name and the ward number. "I hear you've had a little trouble yourself."

She began to cry. Tears coursed down her cheeks, she could hear herself making a thick, rasping sound, her chest hurt with the effort to stifle it.

"This is maybe not the best time," he said, as if she weren't making that awful noise, as if everything were perfectly fine, "but obviously that's the end of your mother as a sitter for the kids. She told me she's known about her heart condition since October and just couldn't bring herself to tell you." Christine had managed to stop the noise in her throat and chest, and though water still spread down her cheeks, it didn't seem to her that she was crying.

"He's your son, too," she said. "Come back and help me. Please." She had not imagined that she would ever beg him to return, and she wondered now if that was all that he'd been waiting for. On the other end of the line, though, there was only silence. "Graeme?" she said finally. He didn't reply, but she heard him draw in a long breath and expel it slowly. Was there someone else in the room with him?

She waited, then slowly put the phone down. She blew her nose, wiped her wet cheeks, and after another moment spent motionless, eyes closed, forcing herself to breathe deeply, she called the operator, asked for the hospital, and when she reached it, for the ward where her mother lay alone and gravely ill. When the nurse told her that her mother was out of danger and could have visitors in the morning, Christine almost began crying again.

"Tell her I love her," she said and hung up quickly. She knew she should call the babysitter, but decided it was too late, she would only wake her.

She rose then and left the office, remembering to flick off the lights and to close the door. As soon as she emerged, Brother Gerald shuffled toward her from where he'd been waiting a discreet distance from the door. She followed him down that hall and then the next until he stopped and opened a door into one of the bare guest rooms. Someone had already put her boots on the spotless rubber mat inside, and wiped her briefcase and set it on the desk across the room.

"Breakfast is at seven." He went shuffling and shaking away.

Christine shut the door and sat down on the bed. The light was so bright it hurt her eyes, but looking around she saw there was no lamp, only the single, bare overhead bulb. She listened, but there was no sound at all, only that odd stillness she'd noticed before in the monastery. Not mere silence as much as it was an intensity in the air, as if the air itself had consciousness. There was a pain in her chest, and she straightened her back, hoping to relieve it.

Was she responsible for her mother's heart attack? She supposed she was. All her mother wanted was that she put Aaron in a special home, at least part of the time, and she would not even consider that. She pictured her mother lying in her hospital bed, electrodes fixed to her chest, a monitor beside her with its line of steady blips, then cast about frantically for another picture to erase that one.

She found herself thinking about Peter Wilmer, that easygoing, apparently uncomplicated man she'd hoped to have a drink with earlier. What if they married? Would they have children of their own? What kind of lover would he be? She thought that perhaps she wasn't sure any more what love was, although it was true that she loved her children, who would both be asleep now, oblivious to the fact that their grandmother was too ill to care for them any more, that their father would not return to them. That from here on, nothing would be the same. She bent her head and clasped it in both hands to stop the chaos expanding inside.

"Nothing bad has happened," she said out loud. "Nothing too terrible has happened."

She put her hands together, then pushed them flat against her breasts and rocked with the pain of her self-hatred, her humiliation, her unextinguished need. For a long time she rocked, pressing her hands against her own small breasts, until finally she felt she could breathe again. She put her hands down to rest, palms flat, on the cheap blue bedspread and sat a long time without moving. The sparseness of the room comforted her. She wondered what it was the monks said when they chanted: *Relinquish, relinquish, relinquish ...* Was that what it was?

Thirsty, she looked around for a water glass without finding one, although now she saw a sink against the far wall. And she was hungry, too, she'd had no dinner. It struck her as bitterly amusing that even now she was hungry and thirsty. She rose and went out into the deserted, silent hall. Her back and neck ached, the muscles of her legs hurt with each step, even her hands hurt—she must have been clenching them. Hardly noticing she had, she went straight to the dining room without one wrong turn.

The end nearest the kitchen was lit by old-fashioned brass wall sconces that gave off a dim but warm pinkish light. She saw that, as she'd hoped, the coffee urn was still hot, and a plate of oatmeal cookies sat under plastic wrap next to it. She poured herself coffee and extracted a cookie from under the wrap. The hall was empty, but she chose to sit in the shadows near the back, where anyone entering would not readily notice her. She needed to think, or to not-think; she needed to wait and get back her strength.

Now when she listened, she could hear only the hum of the fridges in the kitchen and the muted moan of the wind outside the thick walls. It troubled her that she couldn't *hear* the silence, as she'd been able to do only moments earlier. It had surprised her, even thrilled her, although she didn't know how or why. She hoped she had not lost that too, and it seemed now no small thing to her if she had.

Now she heard something. It was the monks, they were chanting again, their voices rising and falling, now loud, now soft, now a tenor voice lifting the sound, now bass again. She couldn't make out the words, realized finally that they were Latin, a language of which she knew nothing. The sound was growing louder, and puzzled, she stood.

In the intensity of her listening, shutting out the room, the darkness, the sound of the wind faint on the other side of the thick walls, Aaron appeared before her, his small face with the long eyelashes, his perfect mouth, his large hazel eyes. How she had kissed him and loved him and cared for him and whispered sweet sayings in his ear, and sung little songs to him. For years now she'd done these things every day, and he had not, not even once, smiled in a way she could be sure was for her, had not held out his arms to be lifted by her, had not pursed those perfect lips to kiss her cheek. Nor had he ever said "Mother" to her, nor "Mom," nor "Mommy." He was a blank wall, yes, and Graeme was right: on the other side there was only an empty room. Did that mean she should not love him?

Now there was the muffled thump of feet striking the floor in unison, and over that sound, as it drew closer, she could hear a rhythmic, dull-metallic *clink, clink, clink*. First the abbot, then a dozen monks walking two by two, entered the dining hall through the door at the far end. They passed the coffee urns, the first row of long, scarred tables and the wooden chairs that lined it on each side. Immediately behind the abbot Christine's student, Richard, followed. He was gowned like the other monks in a dark robe tied loosely at the waist with a cord. She was faintly shocked to see him. He was swinging a censer from which, with each *clink*, a thin stream of pale grey scented smoke rose, which spread toward her and backward so that the monks were partially obscured in a soft cloud, as if they were not yet fully materialized, or were on their way into dissolution. They glanced neither left nor right, chanting as they moved to one side of where Christine stood, the sound of the censer falling back against its chain, repeating itself in rhythm with their swaying forward movement.

As the monks drew nearer, Christine saw there was a door hidden by shadows near where she stood that opened into an unknown part of the monastery, and that this was where the abbot was leading his procession. As they came abreast of her, the abbot turned, and with the edge of his hand made a sign of the cross, casting a blessing toward her.

Then they were gone through the door, their voices fading into the muffled keen of the blizzard still raging outside.

Keeping House

Beth had been worrying about her daughter Janice for some time. Nothing unusual had happened, it was just something in her voice during their regular Sunday phone calls, a kind of tension tempered by sadness, so when Janice phoned on a Thursday, as Beth was finishing the breakfast dishes, she was less surprised than suddenly filled with foreboding.

"Gerry and I are divorcing." Beth couldn't think of anything to say, and miscalculating, she sat down with a bump on one of her oak kitchen chairs. "I doubt you're surprised, Mom," Janice said. "You must have seen things weren't working out."

"I *am* surprised," Beth said, they hadn't been married two full years. "I knew you haven't been quite yourself, but I thought—I don't know what I thought."

"We can't talk to each other, we don't want the same things, he seems to be going in some direction I can't make sense of. I never expected this when we got married." Confused, Beth wanted to ask if Gerald was abusive, or violent, or if he had a girlfriend, or—was Janice having an affair? Finally, she asked, "Is this—mutual?"

"Yes!" Janice said loudly, and then more softly, "Yes," again so that Beth could hear her relief, her desire to leave and go anywhere, now. "He's a nice guy, Mom, but we can both see where this is leading. So we're going to bail out before we start to hate each other. Before we get all entangled ..." In the unfinished sentence Beth saw Duncan turning his back on her, walking away from her and the car loaded with her belongings. Quickly, she said, "Do you need me to come? I'll come right away—"

"Oh, no," Janice said. "I mean, I appreciate the thought, Mom, but really, I'm fine. Will you tell Dad for me?"

Beth had been planning to bundle up and walk to the grocery store for milk and bread as soon as she finished the dishes. This was her regular morning exercise, marching briskly down the shovelled and well-scraped suburban sidewalks, breathing in the bracing winter air. Now, feeling a little strange, although she couldn't have said just how, she poured herself the last cup of coffee, instead, and tried to come to terms with what she'd just heard.

She suspected she was more upset than she ought to be, knowing, as she felt fairly sure she did, that Janice would be all right. She supposed this was because the news brought back memories of her own divorce twenty-six years ago now. Janice and Jeff, the children of her current marriage, were twenty-four and twenty-two. And maybe she was just a little bit angry with her daughter? And if so, why? she asked herself. Because—because—and she remembered how, after her own first marriage had broken up, she'd gone weeks that stretched into months with a pain in her chest that wouldn't go away, that it had taken her years to admit was the literal pain of a broken heart, that—yes, it was true—she'd been close to committing suicide, that even now, today, she doubted she was fully recovered from what her divorce had done to her. And here was Janice, simply walking away, no harm done, no pain suffered. It did make her angry, and she had to laugh, rueful that at her age, her first marriage so far in the past, she still could be such a fool.

She found she now craved her morning walk, and she went to the closet and pulled on her snowpants, her parka, and boots and left the house. Trudging down the sidewalk past the small bungalows that lined the street, she began to study them as if she hadn't been passing them every day for years. Some were still decorated for Christmas even though it was two weeks past, and she realized now why Janice and Gerry hadn't come home for it. At the corner was the pale blue house she could never see without an inward shudder.

One summer afternoon, years earlier, she'd been passing with Jeff in his stroller and Janice holding onto the handle, when a woman, looking to be slightly older than Beth and wearing shorts and a T-shirt, had come out the back door, knelt in the flower bed at the side of the house, and begun weeding. A moment later a boy of about ten, also wearing shorts and a T-shirt, came out and stood beside her. It was their faces that held Beth—their expressions contained such misery that she couldn't look away. Just as Beth and the children were almost opposite the house, the front door opened, a man came briskly out, his face set grimly, and strode to where the woman knelt and the boy stood at the flower bed. He reached toward the woman, the boy stepped between them, there was a wordless struggle, the woman starting to rise, the boy grasping his father's forearm, the man shoving the boy to break his grasp so that the child fell hard, full-length, onto the lawn, and then the husband stepping over the boy and striding away down the other side of the house.

Beth hadn't known what to do. Call the police? Call to the woman and the boy to ask if she could help? Instead, appalled and full of some emotion she couldn't quite identify—fear? shame?—she averted her eyes, at least partly not to let woman and boy know there'd been a witness to their humiliation, and kept going.

The house had changed hands a couple of times since then, and she'd never seen that family again. She hoped the woman had had the sense to take her son and leave before worse harm was done. But remembering the look on her face, the way she seemed less afraid than terribly sad, and yet somehow resigned or patient about what was happening, Beth knew that the woman would never leave. But she often wished that she'd walked up the sidewalk to the two of them and offered help.

At least Duncan had never abused her. That was what she'd told people whether they asked or not, over the years. He never laid a finger on me, she'd told her parents and her siblings and her friends—later, when she began to have friends again. But she wouldn't think about it; it was stupid to still occasionally catch herself thinking about it.

At dinner that night she broke the news of Janice's divorce to Hugh. For a long time he said nothing, seeming stunned by it, and she watched his face grow slowly old, lines that the low light of the dining-room chandelier had faded reappearing in his forehead and around his mouth.

"I thought they were happy," he murmured, and raised his eyes to meet Beth's across the half-eaten casserole, the salad bowl, and their empty wineglasses. She had a sudden intuition that he had wondered if some fatal flaw of Beth's, who was already divorced when he met her, had surfaced in their daughter. She could see him erasing the notion as quickly as it arrived.

"She says they aren't happy together, that it was a mistake, nothing else," Beth told him, her voice gentle, as if she were explaining something sad about life to a child.

"Nothing else?—" he said. "A marriage is nothing—"

"I was glad," Beth said. "I don't want her to suffer, and if she's not suffering—"

"If she's not suffering," Hugh said, "either she's lying or there's something wrong with her." When Beth didn't respond, he went on. "Remember the wedding? Remember?" His voice was louder now and colour was returning to his face. Beth remembered now too: the long intimate gazes into each other's eyes, their hands clasped tightly together, the endlessly long kiss at the altar, and at the head table during the reception, kiss after kiss, while the guests clapped and laughed and clattered spoons against their glasses.

"I always said," Beth remarked, "that no matter how much people think they do, no one knows what goes on inside a marriage." Before she could stop herself, she was back inside her own first marriage, Duncan browbeating her over something she'd said or done that she herself wasn't even able to remember. Or, she thought now, that had never happened, that he invented because he seemed to hate me so much.

"What's wrong?" Hugh asked.

"It's just—Janice and Gerry," she said, not looking at him. But she could feel his eyes held on her face.

"It's natural that old memories would surface at a time like this," he told her gently. Beth lowered her head, unable to look at him.

"I think you should go to her," he went on, lifting his fork and setting it down again against the pale tablecloth.

"But I offered to. She was adamant that I shouldn't come, that she doesn't need me."

"Never mind," Hugh told her. "Go anyway. Go tomorrow."

"I'm supposed to work at the nursing home tomorrow afternoon."

"Get somebody to work for you."

"It's just that she said—"

"I know," he said. "But how clearly can she be thinking? Go to her and see for yourself."

As soon as she arrived at the bus station in the city she called Janice at work to give her a little warning.

"I'm staying at a hotel," she told her. "I don't want to be—I don't want to make matters worse."

"Don't be ridiculous, Mom," Janice said, sounding like an exasperated parent. "Gerry's moved out. Come to the apartment. I'll leave now and meet you there."

The apartment had been half emptied of furniture. There was still the sofa and coffee table, and a small television set standing on a folding TV table instead of the elaborate wall unit that had been there the last time Beth had visited, and there were a couple of whiter rectangles of space on the white wall where pictures had once hung. The kitchen looked much the same, although now there were only two chairs at the small maple table instead of four, and the wedding-present microwave was missing from the counter.

"I told him to take it," Janice said, noticing her mother glancing at the empty spot framed by crumbs. Janice and Gerry both had careers, they had little time for housekeeping. "This weekend I plan to take stock. I might even move. You can help me figure it all out," she said to her mother, casting a smile at her over her shoulder as she opened the fridge door to put away some of the few groceries Beth had brought. Beth had barely registered the briefness of the smile before the fridge's emptiness, its gleaming white walls, struck her with a pang of grief. She'd arrived alone in this very city with only her clothing, a couple of paintings, some books to be unloaded into three bare, white-walled rooms like Janice's, but hers without so much as a bed in it or even a chair to sit down on. And Duncan's cheque in her purse that she couldn't bear to look at.

She had been too numb even to cry, and that pain in her chest had spread and spread until it filled her throat and her abdomen …

"Mom! What's wrong?" Janice was staring into her face with a worried expression. "You're not sick, are you?"

Beth said, "I came here to make sure you're all right," and she laughed, embarrassed, turning away, taking off her coat and going to the closet at the front door to hang it up.

From the kitchen Janice called, "Should we just have omelettes for supper? And you brought a bottle of wine. Great!"

That night, sleeping on the wide living-room couch, refusing Janice's insistent offer of what was now the only bed in the apartment, Gerry having taken the one in the spare room, Beth had a dream; a strange, confusing dream that, although it wasn't a nightmare, troubled her enough to wake her, and for a long time she couldn't go back to sleep.

In the morning, trying to tell Janice about it, she found she couldn't get its images clear or convey its impact, which had been considerable.

"I was walking in a jungle, I think it was, or a forest like in Stanley Park in Vancouver." Janice said, "Mmmm," glancing at the newspaper folded on the table beside her. "It was very dark and I couldn't see my way. There was somebody with me or behind me, I think. A man. I think it was your father, or else maybe it was my first husband—Duncan."

"Duncan," Janice's voice overlapped Beth's. "God, Mom, how old is that marriage anyway? And you're still dreaming about him?" Flustered, Beth laughed in embarrassment.

"I'm sorry," she said. "I'm supposed to be here to check you out." She smiled apologetically at her daughter. "Your father wants to make sure you're okay."

"Do I look like I'm in trouble?" Janice asked. She glanced down quickly, before Beth could read anything in her lively brown eyes, so unlike Beth's own, which were hazel and deep-set, and which she knew often held a puzzled, faintly worried look.

"Would you tell me if you were?" For a long moment Janice said nothing. Beth could see some resistance leaving her, her face grew softer, and her shoulders lowered barely perceptibly.

"I miss him," she said. "And I feel—bad—you know? Because we thought we really loved each other, and it's so … empty without him." She lifted both her hands and pressed their heels against her eyes. "Tell me I'll get over this," she said, her voice muffled. Beth wanted to hold her daughter against her breasts, to smooth her gleaming dark hair and kiss away her tears, but she knew better than to move. Janice put down her hands. "You're still not over Duncan—"

"I was married to him for eight years," Beth said gently. "I left my home, my job, my family and friends, I moved into his community. On the farm we could never escape each other. We were both there, all the time. And he—"

"He was cruel to you," Janice said, softly.

"I've never said that," Beth said.

"You never said anything," Janice said, suddenly sharp. "But we always knew, all of us, when you were thinking about him. He was part of all our lives, even though none of us ever met him." She laughed in a surprised way, as if she'd just realized this, and found the realization amusing in a woeful, world-weary way. "And Dad used to say, 'Leave your mother alone, give her some space.'"

Beth could feel a flush rising up her neck, and her knuckles, newly slightly arthritic, began to ache, a faint, low-level pain that was, nonetheless, a kind of suffering. She wanted to be angry, she thought how good it would be to be angry, to break dishes and scream terrible things, maybe even obscenities, if she could think of any, but she never had done any of these things, and now seemed hardly the time to begin. She took refuge in getting the coffee pot and refilling both their mugs.

"It's Saturday, you don't have to go to work. Let's go shopping for a microwave and a new TV stand."

"Let's go to the big mall," Janice said. "I haven't been there since we got married. Gerry hates malls and especially that one, it's so noisy and crowded." She pulled her thick hair back from her face. "Maybe I could get my hair done, something new. Mmmm?"

"We can have lunch there, make a day of it," Beth said, forcing gaiety into her voice, as she knew Janice had just done.

Beth's dream had been weighted with such mystery that, simple as it was, she couldn't forget it, nor go back to sleep: night in an enormous, endless forest of huge, tall trees, so that she made her way in darkness, yet without stumbling on protruding roots or undergrowth. And a man following her, a husband, although she couldn't be sure which one it was, or even if it was one of the men she'd been married to in real life. About three a.m. she got up quietly, intending to make herself a cup of herbal tea. A shaft of light glowed under Janice's door, and seeing it, Beth knocked softly. She heard a murmured "Come in."

"Can't sleep?" she asked.

"I'm having trouble these days," Janice admitted. Beth could see the dark smudges under her daughter's eyes and a tight sheen to her cheeks that made her suspect she had been crying. "You're not sleeping either?" Janice asked Beth.

"I think it was *American Beauty*," Beth answered ruefully. In the late afternoon they'd passed the mall's movie theatres and, their feet and legs aching, and in unspoken agreement of their disinclination to return to Janice's desolate apartment, they'd bought tickets and gone in. "What an ending."

"I think in real life he'd have been more likely to shoot himself," Janice said in a thoughtful tone.

"I hated the way the Annette Bening character was treated," Beth said. "Like all the ills of Amercan society are the fault of women. She was the only character you never got to empathize with." Beth had sat down on the chintz-covered armchair next to the bed. At its foot she could see the square indentation in the rug of a missing bedtable. Janice set her book down on the white eyelet quilt and pushed her pillows up against the headboard, pulling herself to a sitting position. She was wearing a blue T-shirt with a faded, unreadable message across her small breasts and Beth's heart gave a little lurch, so that she looked away, quickly, before Janice noticed.

"I think I'll make myself a cup of tea. Want one?" Janice asked.

"I'll do it," Beth said, but neither of them moved. They sat on in drowsy silence, each thinking her own thoughts. Outside, in the city, there was only a deep, lulling hush, as if in all the world only they two were awake.

"When I was married to Duncan," Beth said, conscious of the way that Janice was suddenly perfectly still, listening with her whole body, "I used to do the public health flu shots in some of the rural communities around the farm. One time I had to go to the farthest-away, most-isolated hamlet in the whole area. The nurse who usually did that community was sick, so they sent me. I was supposed to be finished by five and home by seven, but it was winter and a storm came up and I couldn't leave." She was staring at the rug and, without noticing she was doing it, she pulled her dressing gown more tightly across her chest. "So an older woman who'd been helping me—she wasn't a nurse, she was making coffee for the people who came in for shots, and showing them where to sit, and if they were really old, making sure they were okay before she let them leave—she said I'd better stay overnight at her house." She turned her head to Janice, explaining, "The village was so small there wasn't a hotel or a motel and the blizzard was blowing so hard you couldn't see across the street. And there were snowbanks everywhere, it was getting dark—" She stopped and drew in a long breath through her nostrils, mouth closed, and went back to fingering her dressing gown, her eyes returning to the rug.

"Mom—" Janice began.

"And so I went to her house. It was a small, old frame house, but very neat and well kept. We went into the living room. It was an ordinary room, hand-crocheted afghans covering the sofa and chairs, lace doilies on the coffee table. A little worn, maybe, but very clean. Her husband was reading a book in an easy chair, in the lamplight. She introduced me to him. He was a nice-looking man, maybe in his sixties, he said hello, but he didn't get up. We two women cooked supper together and the three of us ate. Then we all went back to the living room and sat down. I remember we didn't put the television on until it was time for the news. We just sat there and tried to make conversation. As soon as the news was over I went to bed. I didn't sleep much. In the morning the storm was over and I went home …" In the pause she could feel the intensity of Janice's listening. "A couple of weeks later Duncan and I were eating breakfast and the radio was on and the announcer said that there'd been a murder-suicide in—in that little village where I'd stayed overnight. And Duncan said, teasing me, 'You were there a whole day. Who was it?' And I said—I named that couple I'd stayed with. I was just half joking, you know?" She turned to Janice. "But staying there had been—awful—just awful, the woman was so afraid of the man, she hardly dared to speak to him, and when she did he wouldn't look at her, but he'd cut her off. And she'd get this little rim of sweat around her hairline—"

"Mom—" Janice began again.

"Just these little beads of sweat," Beth said, touching her own temple. "And it turned out it was them. He'd shot her and then, I guess when he realized what he'd done, he killed himself." Janice gasped.

"How horrible!" She hesitated. "But how weird that you should have been there."

"I can't explain that," Beth said in a serious voice, as if Janice had expected an explanation. "I often think of it, although I've never been back to that village. Not once." Tears had crept into her eyes and now they spilled down her cheeks. "I never told Hugh that—I mean, that I was there—or anybody else that I can remember," she said. "I don't know why not."

Janice spoke carefully, as if she were afraid that this was a question her mother might not like. "How long was it after that before you and Duncan split up?"

"What? Oh—" Beth thought. "It was the same year. That was in the late fall and I left the farm this time of year, after Christmas." Realizing why Janice had asked this, Beth turned quickly to her. "I was never in danger of being shot by Duncan. I certainly never thought that I was."

"Still," Janice said, "he did you serious damage, I think."

"It wasn't all his fault," Beth said. "I thought when we got married that I didn't have to be a person any more, or else that he'd show me how, or something. He had such ... charisma, such fearlessness. Things I didn't have myself and didn't know how to get. I mean, I gave myself over to him. I gave him my whole life, I kept nothing back. And that was stupid and wrong. It took me a long time to figure that out."

"If he mistreated you, how can it be your fault?" Janice

asked, the hint of exasperation returning to her voice, so that Beth knew that Janice hadn't understood, or didn't want to understand what Beth had just told her. "You weren't cheating on him or mistreating him in any way, I'm sure. I know you, Mom. You'd never do anything like that. So if he mistreated you, it wasn't your fault." But then, Beth thought, if after so many years of struggling, I finally understand that myself, I also know that understanding isn't enough, that there has to be more for me to figure out about how I was then. And the dark forest of her dream returned to her, so that she put her hand against her eyes and then put it down again.

"He *was* often very cruel," she said calmly, as if they were still discussing the movie. "He would berate me, and I would apologize—for things I hadn't done, that I knew I hadn't done, or that I knew he'd done, not me—just to get peace. Just to get us back together again. I'd say to myself, How important is this quarrel, anyway? Did I want to end up divorced? To have to be without him," she said, turning to Janice, seeing the wonder in her eyes as she stared back at her mother, "was unthinkable to me. Beyond unthinkable. And so I'd abase myself for what I thought was the sake of our marriage." She laughed. "And wound up divorced anyway."

"My God," Janice said.

"I was—foolish?" Beth said, frowning, leaning forward in her chair as if she meant to rise. "Or—something," she said finally. It seemed to her that she'd said too much, gone too far with her own daughter, that this kind of thing was better said to priests or psychiatrists. Not that she ever had.

Janice said, "I've got an empty spot where Gerry was"—she touched her chest with clasped hands—"and it's very painful. But it sounds to me like he hollowed you right out. No wonder you can't get over it."

Beth wanted to protest that she was over it, had been over it for years; her life was what it was and she would continue to carry her own history quietly, as she had been doing all this time. But when she looked over to her small, dark-haired daughter, appearing now so much like a sleepy child in the too-large, rumpled bed, she felt only shame that she was so little comfort to her. Surely she knew something; surely she had something to tell her. A truck moaned by, on a street far off from their building, and Beth stirred and sat forward again, conscious of the passage of time, that she had to hurry. The words were coming to her now.

"Soon you will begin to fill that emptiness with friendships," she said. She'd begun thoughtfully, but her voice began to take on clarity, grew a little louder and more firm. "In a couple of years you'll be married again, time will pass and you'll remember Gerry only once in a long while, if you do at all, because you'll have small children to look after, and a house you and your new husband are filling with things you like, that you choose together. Maybe you'll be back at work, part-time at least, and your life will be full and rich. Gerry will become merely a tiny part of all that richness. There will be no emptiness at all any more."

Janice said nothing, her dark eyes fixed on her mother, filled with wonder, perhaps with a tinge of hope. Beth's voice hung on, scintillating on the thick and still air as if she had spoken from some other world than this small bedroom in this half-emptied apartment in the middle of a city Beth had long ago, for a few lonely years, called home.

On the long bus ride back in the rapidly descending winter twilight Beth remembered her dream about the forest and the man following her. She thought about Duncan and a longing to put away that part of her life forever overcame her and she almost wept, not just for herself, but for Janice and for what seemed to her now the sadness of human life. The bus carried only a few passengers and as the twilight turned to darkness everyone seemed to be drowsing, their heads and shoulders swaying with the bus's hypnotic motion.

Beth's dream began to seem real, perhaps by now she was asleep, and she was back in the forest, the thick-trunked, heavy-limbed black trees towering over her, enclosing her, as she moved slowly, searching for a way out. Ahead, glimpsed between foliage-covered branches, she saw a glimmer that she felt sure was a flicker of sunlight shining on a grassy meadow.

She hurried forward, but as she drew nearer to the patch of light, she began to see that instead of a ray reflected from a green, flower-dotted meadow, it came from a wall: tall, solid, impenetrable, extending both directions in the shadowed depths of the forest. She saw that she could not climb over it, that there was no door through it, nor could she go around. For a long time she crouched, trembling, below it, sweat dampening her body, her heart full of terror and longing. Finally, she looked back the way she had come, and beyond that, into the darkest part of the forest, into the trackless wilderness where she had never been. She saw it was a place she had no choice but at last, alone and resolutely, to go.

Random Acts

This is perhaps not a story to tell, she thinks. Then, no, this is perhaps the *only* story to tell. It's the story of how she was raped, when she was maybe thirty-one or thirty-two, and how all the bad things that ran wordlessly through her culture about herself and about women as a species flooded over her and she blamed herself and was ashamed and never told anybody till she felt securely beyond her youth.

Not that it helped. By then she had gone too far for rage, too far for thoughts of beatings, castration, murder, or a life lived without men. What she thinks, increasingly, glumly, since that first telling of it, is there was nothing she could have done about it then, and there's still nothing she can do about it. In fact, she's just grateful he didn't break any bones, subduing her easily with his weight and implacability, so that she acquiesced as the only way to avoid being hurt. Nor did he force her to any act of extreme perversion that would have haunted her dreams for the rest of her life. Even her children weren't in the house, but away, visiting their grandparents. Yes, she thinks, I was very lucky.

Not that she doesn't see the irony of her conclusion. As far as she knows, she was the only one he followed home that night, she was the only one he raped. But for years she didn't even call it rape. She didn't call it anything, she didn't even think about it. One night she was sitting talking about a mutual friend with a man she'd just met that day, when she heard herself say calmly, conversationally, "That was the night I was raped."

Since then she's been thinking about it a lot, going over all the details one by one, as far as she can remember, since it happened twenty-five years before. Stop that, she tells herself. If you doubt each detail as you remember it, you'll soon doubt that you were raped at all. And she remembers the ugly muscles of his upper arms and the way he pushed her, relentlessly, inexorably, till he was inside the house, then in the bedroom, then lying on the bed on top of her.

She doesn't understand why she didn't feel like the woman she'd seen in a television movie who'd been raped and who went a little crazy afterward, took a dozen baths and was afraid to go out at all and then set up a trap for the man, inviting him over, planning to say, "Come in," when he knocked on her door, and then to blast him with a shotgun. And there were other stories too, in magazines and on radio and television, about women reacting to rape. She'd found them all excessive and self-aggrandizing, reactions of women who couldn't have been too stable to begin with, who clearly harboured some very bad notions about themselves as sexual beings. For years that was what she thought.

But the older she gets, clutching her secret to herself, the less sure she is that those women were wrong, and that her reaction—to keep silent, not to think about it, to count herself lucky among those who'd been raped—is perhaps the less rational approach after all, and that maybe *she* is the one who values herself too little, who suffers from an absence of self-esteem and a badly developed sexuality. They'd been outraged at their violation; she hadn't even been surprised. She'd resisted till she saw resistance was useless, then she'd gone limp till he was done. All those years, whenever it popped into her mind, she'd quickly thought of how she was lucky compared to being a concubine or being forced to commit suttee or being a tribal slave. Even now, when she's learned to value herself quite a lot, she's still not outraged and isn't sure why not.

And, she tells herself, if you never told anybody, you can hardly be the only raped woman who reacted that way. Remember dating when you were a college student? Most dates wound up in wrestling matches. You expected them, there was an unspoken accord: he would try, you would say no, at a certain point you'd either give in or he would realize you meant it and stop. Sometimes he went further than the accord allowed, and if he did, you didn't go out with him again. It was a dangerous game, but the only one. Now she thinks that maybe she'd been lucky there too and her girlfriends were being raped and not telling anyone.

Besides, the only reason she didn't give in was that her mother had told her she shouldn't, so had the nuns and priests who'd educated her, and her girlfriends, and even the boys who were her friends, counselling her sagely and whispering about girls they all knew who were easy. If you didn't resist, it was absolutely clear, the life you were being groomed for would be over, and that was a price too high for anybody to pay.

Then, abruptly, when she was in her late twenties and newly divorced, all that ended. Suddenly, making love was socially acceptable, a positive good, everybody was doing it, it was expected. She thinks that probably almost nobody was doing it as much as they implied they were—she, for one, wasn't—but the point was that you could if you wanted to and nobody would call you a slut or a whore or easy. Nobody would say anything at all.

I never even noticed him, she thinks. A dozen of them together in a club at one big table, her girlfriends, somebody's husband, a few male friends who were always around, and him, the rapist, a stranger, a house guest of one of the men. They hadn't even sat close together. When she thought about that night, she remembered he'd sat on the opposite side of the table at the far end, and when she thought harder about it, she'd remembered he'd asked her to dance, that he hadn't been a good dancer, that they'd danced once, then sat down. She hadn't even talked to him, and she hadn't liked him because he was so silent and his silence had a heavy impenetrableness to it that made her wonder why he'd asked her to dance.

The reason she didn't at first remember dancing with him was that sitting at a table behind them was a man she'd had an affair with and, in a forlorn way, was still in love with. He was sitting with a woman; by the way he was acting she could tell he was in love. When she'd noticed him and smiled and waved, he'd deliberately looked away without even nodding. She'd been so wounded by this unexpected, deliberate, and undeserved slight that all enjoyment was leached from the evening, and after a while, it was barely midnight, she'd gotten up, said goodnight, and left.

But then, she thinks, I do remember that the man I'd danced with stood up when he noticed I was leaving, that as I was walking away he was hastily trying to make change to settle his share of the bill. And I hurried out of the club, and I kept telling myself he wasn't leaving because of me. And yet, as I passed the shadowed street behind the club, I thought seriously of stepping into it and hiding against a building till he'd gone by. I didn't, my training to stay on well-lit streets was too strong, and besides, I kept thinking I was imagining things, that he wasn't going to follow me, or if he was, it was only because my house and the house he was staying in were near each other.

Even now, after all these years, after all the times she's

remembered the details of that night, she can still see the comforting shadows of that narrow side street. She remembers clearly how she hesitated, how close she came to taking those few quick steps that would have saved her, and how she didn't, telling herself not to be silly, not to be melodramatic.

I never told anyone, she thinks, because if I did, how could I maintain my dignity, my good name, my social standing as a decent woman? I was a divorcée, I was in a nightclub unescorted, I'd had affairs, I'd slept with men I'd just met. I'd violated all the codes I was raised with, had become all the things a dozen years before I'd fought with my dates not to become. This is why for twenty-five years I couldn't tell this story. Because it was all my fault; I had been asking for it.

Is that why I refused to think about it? she asks herself. Because I couldn't face that awful truth? That everyone would think I should have expected it, given my lifestyle? That because of it nobody would care? She knows that was part of it: her pride kept her silent, and her stubborn belief in her own strength to endure even the worst that fate might have in store for her.

For all those years she hasn't allowed herself to think about it, except inadvertently, stopping herself as soon as she noticed she was. Now, her dark secret out in the open at last, she's driven obsessively to remember it clearly, in every detail. Despite the new climate of opinion, she still suspects it really was her fault, as she'd thought for all these years, something she'd earned, and has no right to be troubled or angry about. She needs to know the truth about it, either to accept the blame or to at last feel the outrage she's told she has a right to.

No, it's more than that, she thinks. She's reached a time when she needs to study her rape from every possible angle in order to at last discover its true meaning; she's driven to gathering together all the details of her life, every single one. She's

weaving them into a precise tapestry—her finished life—
something, when she reaches old age, she'll be able to glance
at with awe and in contentment, everything sorted and in its
place, all passions wiped away, everything clearly what it is and
nothing more.

She knows that what happened to her was trivial compared
to the rapes other women have endured. She wasn't even really
frightened, not at any time during the whole thing. He scared
me, the way when I got my key out he stood close to me, and
when I tried to slip inside first and shut the door on him, he put
his leg in the gap, shoved, and was inside. Then I was scared,
she thinks, but not terrified, just scared, because I knew he
would try to force me to have sex. I didn't think beyond that,
because he was a close friend of a man I trusted, and I couldn't
believe anybody that man cared about would be capable of
anything really bad like maybe—murder. As he pushed his way
in, I believe I clung to that thought.

She remembers he put his arms around her and kissed her in
the darkness of her living room—I don't remember anything
about that part, she tells herself—and said, "Where's the
bedroom?" He thought it was upstairs and was pushing her
toward it and she said, "No, not upstairs," thinking if he
couldn't find the bedroom she'd be safe, but the moon was so
bright and they were at the bottom of the stairs and it was
through the open door beside them, they could see the moonlight shining on the satin spread.

She can't remember exactly about her clothes. She would
have been wearing jeans, she doesn't know how they came off.
She remembers his belt buckle hurting her and him raising up
to undo it while he kept one forearm across her chest. She
fought with him, pushed against him, tried to hold her legs
together, to bring her knees up, to shove him away, but it was
hopeless. In the one effort when she used all her strength to

throw him off, he responded by using his strength to hold her down. She knew when she felt his masculine power that if she didn't stop fighting him, he not only could hurt her, he would. It seemed the only sensible thing to do was to give in.

Somehow the sex didn't matter much, not at the time, anyway. It was horrible and disgusting, but it was his action, not hers, so she wasn't disgusting, he was. That was what she was thinking as it happened, that it wasn't much, it wasn't anything. After, she pretended she was asleep. He pushed her a bit or something, she doesn't clearly remember what, and then he just left. Got up, pulled on his pants, walked out.

She remembers how the second she heard the door shut she leaped off the bed and locked it. She doesn't know if she saw this through the window or if she imagined it, but she sees him hesitate and look over his shoulder when he hears the bolt snap shut. As if it just occurred to him she might be mad at him or afraid of him, as if up to that moment it never occurred to him that she had any feelings at all. Or maybe she was going to call the police. She remembers she thought of them for only one brief instant, shuddering at what they might say to her. No, she never seriously considered the police, but she thinks at that moment it might have crossed his mind, and for an instant *he* was afraid.

Then I just walked around the house in the dark, she remembers, didn't even put on any lights. Just walked around from room to room and looked out the windows at the moonlight. And I felt so bad. I felt that life was too awful to want to live. That I wasn't loved by anyone, that I wasn't—I was going to say, fit to live, she thinks, but that sounds like all those women on TV and radio and in magazines who are so excessive. Anyway, it wasn't quite like that.

I was fighting this terrible sense of loss and the ugliness of life. I would never recover from this because I had been so defiled, and all the things I'd believed in, all the things I'd tried to be, one silent, well-muscled stranger could destroy in a minute. Could make me feel I was a fool, and alien, too, to the loving, clean world I was raised in because I was so bad, so guilty, so big a liar about myself.

Yet, as well as she can remember, she didn't think of suicide. Instead, she'd been plunged down into an echoing underworld whose very air was made of something more resonant and more meaningful than mere pain, and the place was so far down and so dark she couldn't pull herself out of it, couldn't even think of escaping, couldn't think at all. Now she sees it was the place that at bottom holds death, and she sees she'd been aware of it then, but beyond action of any kind.

This is why she feels no outrage, only this bottomless, unending sorrow whenever she thinks of it. That he had no right was never in question, but—if only she could hold onto that glimmer she sometimes catches of some greater wisdom that might tell her what she really wonders: why so small a thing, that didn't even leave a bruise, made her feel so bad.

Eventually she must have simply gone to sleep. The next day she got up and went to work and looked after her children when they returned from visiting their grandparents, and kept on going to work and doing all the things she was supposed to do—doing them badly sometimes, fitfully, failing as often as she succeeded, being an ordinary, normal human being, she supposes, and didn't even try to kill herself.

She regards it also as ironic that the night she heard herself say out loud she'd been raped, the mutual friend she and her new acquaintance had been talking about was the man who'd sat behind her in the club that night, the man she'd been in love with, who'd refused even to say hello. She remembers how his deliberate turning away from her had hurt as much as if he'd slapped her. Even now she can't think why he'd done that, and she's surprised to find it stands out in her memory as one of the worst hurts she's had to endure.

Now she remembers something else that hovered on the edge of her memory all these years. The day afterward, coming home from work to discover she'd forgotten her keys, she'd had to break a pane of glass in the French doors in the dining room to get in. A few nights later a male friend walked her home from the movie she'd been to with her friends. She must have invited him in, because she remembers when he saw the broken glass lying where she'd left it on the dining-room floor, he'd picked up every shard and put it all in the garbage. She remembers the strange way he did it, glancing at her once, not listening to her feeble protest that she'd do it herself in the morning, but bending so quietly and carefully, with an air of the most complete gentleness, a sort of tenderness toward her for which she could find no explanation.

Neither of them spoke as he worked, but it was as if they both knew this was something she was unable to do herself, something she needed help with. Even now she doesn't know why she couldn't do it, and she remembers how as she watched him work she had been filled with gratitude, she nearly wept for his kindness. Yet try as she might, she can't remember his face or his name, only his gentleness, and the sound of his broom brushing over the hardwood floor, sweeping up the last particles of broken glass.

Thief of Souls

Astrid Park heard the news after school on Friday in the district's one grocery store.

"What?" she said, too loudly, in surprise. Then, because the storeowners were known to be in sympathy with the church, she asked softly, "Are you sure?" The woman who'd spoken to her was Chantal's mother. Chantal was in Astrid's grade three class.

"No, it's for real," Mrs. Terry told her, reaching for the broccoli which, as usual, had seen better days. "One of the preacher's kids, Rebekah, told Chantal. Scared her, I can tell you. Eyes as big as saucers!" She shook her head, her lips pursed, and tossed the broccoli back into the bin. This far north it was impossible to get fresh produce.

"And the date?" Astrid asked.

"Next Saturday night," Mrs. Terry told her. "You don't think the world would end on a weekday, do you? Chantal said two in the morning, I think." She dropped a package of limp carrots into her basket. For some time after Mrs. Terry had moved away, Astrid stood staring at the bins of shrivelled and faded vegetables. A lot of the children in the school belonged to the church—God's Saints or Church of Holy Brethren—she wasn't sure which one it was. Maybe their parents would keep them at home the next few days, in view of the fact that the world was going to end on Saturday. If they did, that would set them apart psychologically from the rest of the community, she thought, it would make it easier to calm the others.

She wondered if Warren, the school principal, had heard, and then was sure he had. He'd been in the community fifteen years and knew everybody in town—not hard in a village of fifty—and the country parents as well, since he lived on an acreage a few miles from town, while Astrid, in the middle of her second year here, chose to keep to herself, seeing adults only at parent-teacher interviews, various school ceremonies, and the extracurricular activities she supervised. She didn't even attend the annual fowl supper that absolutely everybody went to. She had no need for society, she told herself, when she thought about it at all, but what she really felt was a kind of horror that she might settle in here and begin to live as everyone else did, that if she did the things they did, she might become just like them.

When she stepped outside carrying her bag of groceries, she saw that it had begun to snow again, as if the town were not virtually buried in snow already. In mid-February the previous winter a newly arrived teacher had simply packed up and left in the middle of the night. It was the snow, old Mrs. Warkentine, Astrid's neighbour who'd been boarding him, told her when Astrid was out shovelling the sidewalk in front of her small frame house. She told Astrid that he'd said he felt like he was suffocating, like they'd all be buried alive.

"Shouldn't of come up here in the first place," the old lady told her. "Everybody knows we get six-eight feet of snow winters."

Putting her two pork chops in the fridge and the wilted head of pale lettuce in the sink to be washed and, hopefully, crisped, she thought of the trouble this new proclamation would cause.

Since she'd been here, the two churches had banded together to have all the Harry Potter books taken out of the school library and then they had gone through all the school's board games and library shelves to weed out every game or book that had anything in it they thought might fall under the rubric of "occult." Even the C. S. Lewis books had gone. Earlier, they had tried but failed to stop the teaching about dinosaurs and the big bang theory of creation. The provincial Department of Education had gotten involved in that one. Everybody not a member of either church was contemptuous of them, but in this very isolated community there were enough of them to wield considerable power. Troubled, she decided to call Warren to see how he thought the teachers ought to handle the decree.

"Oh, yes, I heard it a couple of weeks ago," he told her. "But as there's nothing we can do about it, I put it in my report to the director of ed, and I haven't heard a word since."

"I'm afraid that the children, the young ones anyway, will be upset by it," she said. She could read his lack of reaction only as indifference, and added stiffly, "I feel I need some way of approaching this with my class. Something that won't offend the families involved, but that will calm at least those children who go to a different church." Before he could reply, she threw in, "I seem to be the last to hear."

"No, no," he said quickly, ever the diplomat, so that she knew the other teachers had indeed been talking about it. Her fault, she knew, because she avoided going into the staff room. "Word just started leaking out the last few days." There was another silence. She suggested, "The local school board?"

"Half of them are members of that church," he said. "They'd just tell us to shut down the school and go home and pray." He laughed, and in the sound, careless and distant, she thought she heard annoyance at her and, surprising herself, she felt exasperation, where up until now, no matter what she'd seen happen, or been told about events in the community, she'd felt nothing, was barely interested. And there'd been some stunning events: a proven case of incest, and last winter, a murder-suicide on an isolated farm. Does this mean I'm getting better? she wondered, and wondered too at her own odd choice of language, as if she'd been ill, although she hadn't. Warren said, "I'll think about it, and let you know on Monday what I've come up with."

As she was turning her pork chop in the frying pan she saw through her frosted kitchen window that the snow was still coming down, if anything, thicker than it had been earlier. Everybody was saying it had been years since there'd been so much snow, something to do with global warming, they said. She sighed, thinking of her sidewalk that this winter required cleaning almost every day. But when she rose early to shovel away the snow, she was sometimes rewarded by seeing a moose on the street. Even bears were said to occasionally wander out of the forest into the village, and unseen wolves howled eerily at sundown most days.

She was sitting down to her meal when the phone rang. It seldom rang, she'd had it connected only to be available for school business, and for a moment she thought she wouldn't answer it. But it might be Warren calling back with some new information—maybe the pastor had called off his proclamation—and she rose and lifted the receiver.

"Hello?"

After a moment a distant voice said, "Yes?" Astrid could barely hear this through the heavy, monotonous humming on the line, nor could she tell if the voice was male or female. She thought that it must be long distance, but she'd cut all her ties to the south by going away without telling anyone she was leaving. She'd pointed the car west, having a vague desire for the mountains, but she passed through them without finding the courage to let the car sail out over a canyon, or to crash it into a rock wall. Once through them, she'd turned north and kept driving until she'd reached the road's end at this village of tumbling-down frame shacks, mostly deserted except for those lived in by widows too old to manage any more on their tiny farms, and with the massive, dark spruce forest pushing at its borders. Here she'd rented her little house from a local farmer and moved in, telling no one where she was. All the other teachers, in love with the north as they said, lived on acreages out in the forest or in log houses on the edge of the nearby lake.

Only Lucy Gonnick knew where she was and that was a coincidence: Lucy's husband and a friend on a fishing trip at the lake a hundred miles from here where Astrid had happened to be in the lodge, treating herself to a fresh fish dinner after one of her solitary tramps. But this didn't sound like Lucy. Or did it?

"Hello?" she repeated. There was a long, crackling silence. The voice asked, "Are … all right?"

"Who is this?"

"… worry …" was all she could extract from the static of the reply. Then the line went dead. Frowning, Astrid hung up the phone and went back to her dinner.

"Astrid? Is it you? So this is where you are!" Tom Gonnick had blurted. Then he'd blushed, as if it had just dawned on him that she wasn't glad to see him.

"How is everybody?" she'd asked, struggling to keep her voice even, meaning Lucy and the Woodwards, the two couples she and Donald had been friends with.

"Everybody's fine," he said. "Darcy starts college this fall …" Lucy and Astrid were the same age, thirty-eight, but Lucy and Tom had three children, while Donald and Astrid, meeting and marrying late, had put off having children. Their joy in each other felt complete, they told each other, children could wait. And now, she had left only her memory of him. Tom had fallen silent, brushing one hand over his thinning hair, puzzled and uncomfortable. She didn't ask him to sit down. "You should write," he said. "I mean—Donald—" She'd gazed steadily at him. His voice trailed away.

"It's better this way, Tom," she said. He'd stared down at her for a moment more, then gone away.

At Donald's funeral, small, blonde Lucy had wept so hard, her face smeared with tears she couldn't seem to stop, that Tom had to take her home. Astrid remembered Lucy's blue eyes peering questioningly into hers, but little else about the funeral. Only that she was angry with Lucy for her excessive, even histrionic display, when Astrid herself had been unable to weep a tear, had felt that tears were for the merely broken-hearted, while she was beyond sadness, beyond even despair; she was dead too, like Donald.

But Tom would ask the lodge owner where she'd come from, and would get the answer since she'd rented a cabin from him for the two-month hiatus from school. All through that short northern summer she'd hiked the woods around the lake. The old Indian who worked there had warned her about bears. He'd told her to sing or whistle when she was walking. "Don't think of him when you walk," he told her. "And never call him by name. Call him the Big One, so he won't know you are thinking of him."

At noon on Monday she went in search of Warren and found him in the gym refereeing a junior boys' basketball game. When he saw her in the wide doorway, he gave his whistle to a boy and came to her. She knew she baffled him. He wanted his staff to behave as if they were a family and she kept an unbending distance that he could find no way to breach. She saw him as shallow—doubtless he knew that too—although, she felt, amiable and probably decent-hearted enough.

Before long, nine teachers were crowded into his office, the six women seated on worn wooden stacking chairs, the three men leaning against the fake-pine walls. Dwayne Johansen, perhaps guessing what this emergency meeting was about, was the last to enter, bringing their number to ten. He was tall and very fair, and in the office's unshaded overhead lights, Astrid wondered if he were paler than usual.

"Dwayne," the principal said, "we're going to need your help here." Dwayne said nothing, folding his arms across his chest and staring down past the sharp press of his grey slacks to his polished black oxfords. The other men were wearing scuffed sneakers and shabby corduroy or denim pants. "As we all know, Pastor Vernon has told his parishioners that the world will end on Saturday night at 2:37 a.m." The teachers glanced at each other, holding their faces straight. Somebody snickered. Dwayne nodded once, briskly, without taking his eyes off his shoes. "Mrs. Park, here," Warren went on—oh, of course, he would lay responsibility at her door—"is concerned that this may upset the younger children and that we should have a strategy"— he looked at her when he said this—"to deal with it."

"The school is unusually quiet today, I thought," Raymond Carpentier, the exchange teacher from Quebec, remarked into the silence. He was a slight young man with a thin blond moustache, someone Astrid saw as like herself, although she didn't define this. When they met on the street, they nodded once, then looked away without speaking.

"Yeah, it is," Maisie Rolland said loudly. "I'm going to tell them that the world isn't going to end and they should relax, forget about it." Dwayne Johansen suddenly lifted his head, the light striking his glasses so that his eyes appeared as two eerily shining shields in his face.

"You would be wrong," he said. He lowered his head to let his gaze rest on each of their faces, his eyes sliding past Astrid as if she were beneath his notice. "I ask you to join us in the church Saturday night. We will spend what time is left in prayer there. In fact, we will spend each evening from now on in prayer at the church. You should all join us, for when the Lord sends his fire or his flood or his earthquake to rend this world from end to end, it will not go well with those of you who are unprepared." There was a shocked silence. "Tell the children to come too. That's what I intend to tell my class." He sounded almost cheerful at this last comment.

When still nobody said anything, their eyes riveted on him, he turned and went out, shutting the door quietly behind him. They stirred then and turned back to Warren.

"Good thing he has grade twelves," he said with an easy laugh. "They never listen to anything we tell them."

Appalled, Astrid said, "He has no right to speak to them about his private beliefs! He must be stopped!" She'd been too vehement, she could feel the others carefully not looking at her.

Raymond Carpentier said gently, "Why don't we tell them that different people have different beliefs, and that we—their teachers—don't believe this."

"It's spreading, you know," shy Joyce Rapchuck interjected. "The Dickensons told me they'd be there Saturday night. They said a lot of people were starting to think maybe they should be there too. Just in case, I guess." She laughed in an embarrassed way, clasping her hands tightly and setting them on her lap.

Warren said, "Tell them that people are free to believe what they want, but that doesn't mean they have to believe it. Tell them most people don't believe it, and they should just go on with things the way they always do. I'm sure most of them have already been told that at home."

The teachers began to move out of the office. Astrid said quickly, "And how do we calm the little ones who are bound to be very frightened?"

"Uh, I'll leave that up to you," Warren said. He was rummaging in his desk, beginning to pile books he needed for his next class.

At 3:25, Astrid told her pupils to put away their notebooks and sit quietly because she wanted to talk to them. The ensuing clatter was brief, as if even these young children knew what was coming and were eager to hear it.

"You know that—" she began, when suddenly Erin Molloy raised her hand, her small face drained of colour. Astrid saw that she was ill, and said, "You run to the bathroom. Alice, go with her. I'll be right there." For an instant she'd thought this more urgent, but then, seeing the alarm on several of their faces, she hesitated. "Children," she began, but her carefully prepared words had deserted her. She paused, then said softly, "Don't be afraid. No one else in all of Canada thinks the world is going to end on Saturday."

"The pastor said—" Jody Akinson began.

"I know that, Jody. But perhaps the pastor is wrong." Jody shook her head slowly from side to side in denial, her stiff brown braids scraping each shoulder, her lips clamped tightly in imitation of someone, probably her mother.

"We'll talk some more tomorrow," Astrid told them. "Now sit quietly until the bell rings and then you may go."

In the elementary girls' bathroom Erin was kneeling at a toilet, still retching. Astrid dismissed Alice, soaked a handful of paper towels, and brought them to Erin, helping the child to sit upright on the cold cement floor and wiping her face gently with the wet paper. "There, now," she said. "You're fine now. The Church of Holy Brethren is wrong, you know." Astrid knew Erin's family were Catholics. "Don't listen to Jody," she said. Deafeningly, the last bell of the day rang. Erin said, "I'm going to miss my bus." She got slowly to her feet.

"Maybe I should get someone to drive you home?"

"I have to take the bus," Erin said, twisting her hands, then moving to the door. She seemed steady enough, and colour was returning to her cheeks and lips. While she ran for her backpack, parka, and boots, Astrid hurried to the exit where a row of frosted and snow-covered yellow school buses sat idling, clouds of exhaust billowing up, partially obscuring them. Over the heads of jostling, running children she called through the opened doors to one of the drivers that Erin Molloy had just been ill.

"No wonder!" the woman said angrily. She wore a man's plaid farm cap, the earflaps pulled down. "It's that darn Pastor Vernon, he's got the kids scared to death. I'll watch her," she called, bobbing her head to see around the children climbing onto her bus.

Astrid was preparing her supper when, again, the phone rang. She had just noticed that the handle on her frying pan was cracked, that she needed a new one, which reminded her that her toaster had long since stopped working. Eventually she would have to go on a shopping trip. She hadn't been back to the city since the day after the funeral, when she'd thrown a few things in the car and driven away, leaving behind a cheque and a note for her landlord, asking him to put her furniture in storage. Even now, a year and a half later, the thought of the city roused only a kind of blankness in her, a wall that she couldn't penetrate, that she didn't want to penetrate. She lifted the receiver and heard again the loud humming, and then a crackling that might have been a voice trying to break through the blanket of meaningless sound.

"Lucy?" There was a noise at the other end, paper rustling, or someone changing the receiver from one ear to the other. "I don't want you to call, Lucy," she said, patient now. When there was no answer, she went on. "You know I couldn't stay there without him." It was all she could do to stifle the sounds that wanted to flow out of her, that she had never yet released from the moment she'd opened the door to the policeman and had known at once that the worst had happened, that her life was over. She had been unable to look at Donald's remains; in her place Tom had gone to identify him. Lately, it had crept into her mind that perhaps she'd made a mistake not to go herself. "I don't want to be reminded," she said now. "Can't you understand that? I can't—" She put the receiver down.

Before she got into bed, she scraped frost from her bedroom window and, cupping her hands around her eyes to screen out the interior light, saw that it was still snowing, although less heavily now. Climbing into bed she thought of poor little Erin Molloy, and of the way Jody Akinson's face had closed, as if she were an adult of forty instead of an eight-year-old. This angered her so greatly that she couldn't sleep, and she tossed and turned, trying to think what she might do, until it occurred to her that she herself might go to the pastor. She lay still, thinking over this idea. It seemed clear to her that, for various reasons, no one else would try to reason with him.

She resolved to go the next day. What she would say she wasn't sure: ignore the truth or falsity of his pronouncement in favour of pointing out he had no business frightening young children? Threaten to report him to the child welfare people? She decided she would begin in a quiet, reasonable way, and wait and see how the meeting went.

But on Tuesday morning it was snowing hard again, and while she was shovelling the night's accumulation from the walk that passed her house, adding to the high banks on each side so that she could barely see across the street any more, the idea of going herself to the pastor seemed less appropriate. Why would he listen to her? She had no authority, no meaningful position in the community, she didn't even go to church.

But at ten that morning stern little Jody Akinson, for no apparent reason, began to cry, and when Astrid asked her why she was crying, she merely cried harder, her narrow child's chest convulsing with each sob. Alarmed, Astrid hurried her into the empty nurse's office, set her on a chair, smoothing her hair, wiping her tears with tissues from her pocket, and said, "Listen, Jody. The world is not going to end on Saturday." She was aware of the words popping into her head: *It has already ended*, and the absurdity of this confused her.

"Mom and Dad say it is," the child said. "The pastor, too." Astrid wiped Jody's cheeks with a tissue.

"The pastor has made a mistake," she said, firm now. "Shall I phone your mother to come for you?" Jody nodded yes, then began to cry again, shaking her head no.

"I don't want to go to heaven," she sobbed.

After the school buses had disappeared into the curtain of thickly falling snow, Astrid placed the workbooks to be marked in her canvas bag, pulled on her boots and parka, and left the empty school. There was no wind and as she walked, large soft flakes of snow piled up on her shoulders and woollen hat and the top of her bag. Nor was it too cold, so that she rather enjoyed the trip to the edge of town where the church sat, a converted farmhouse, the dark mass of coniferous forest that surrounded the village nearly touching its back wall, and the lurid crimson sign out front—"Are you saved?"—muted now by the thick fall of snowflakes drifting silently down.

She found the pastor inside taking fat, creamy-yellow candles from cardboard boxes and placing them in holders through the church. The holders were of various sizes and materials, so that Astrid thought they must have come from his parishioners' homes.

"Mr. Vernon?" She was suddenly not sure if this was his first name or his last. He started and turned to her, a candle in each hand. "I'm Mrs. Park, the grade three teacher. I'd like to speak with you."

He set down the candles and came toward her, brushing his hands against his trouser legs, then rolling down the sleeves of his clean white shirt and buttoning the cuffs. He was not much taller than she was, but well built and athletic-looking, and for one who seemed to wield so much power, surprisingly young, perhaps in his mid-thirties. As he came closer, she saw that he was very handsome, that his features were nearly perfect. He fastened his clear, light brown eyes on hers in a too-intense way which seemed to her calculated, annoying her, so that she stared back coldly until he spoke.

"Good to meet you. I've just sent my lady-helpers home to cook supper for their families," he explained, as if it embarrassed him to be found doing the work himself. "Let's go into my office." She followed him and seated herself in the armless wooden chair across from the kitchen table that served as his desk. She was surprised by the ordinariness of his manner, and it occurred to her that given this, he couldn't possibly believe that the world was going to end in only a couple of days. And he looked tired, but the tiredness seemed to be held in abeyance by a kind of jumpy tension. She thought, If you really believed, and if you felt yourself one of the chosen, wouldn't you be serene? Taken aback by this intuition, for a second she didn't know what to say, then decided to be direct.

"I'm told you have convinced your parishioners the world will end on Saturday night." When he didn't respond, staring at her in that same disconcerting, theatrical way, she went on. "I don't for a second believe this or I wouldn't be here. Or, if I believed this, I suppose I'd be helping you prepare for when the lights go out." She wished she hadn't said this latter sentence, and was annoyed that his stare was rattling her, as it was meant to do.

"As they will," he said, "you may be sure of that," and he smiled. "I would say by nightfall on Saturday." Casting about for something to say that wouldn't be merely argumentative, she had been staring at the bookcase on her right, empty except for a few threadbare hymnals. Now she turned her eyes to him to find his expression tinged with dislike—no, disdain— reminding her of Dwayne Johansen's gaze.

"Three of my pupils belong to your church. They are children, and you have frightened them terribly." He tilted his chin upward and she wondered if perhaps he'd flushed, but it was hard to tell. "Not to mention the spillover effect on the others, whom you've no right to frighten either."

"Those of you who do not believe, who do not repent, will be cast into hell for all eternity," he said mildly, even gently, lowering his head to fasten his gaze on her again. "Those who do will soon be joy itself. A little fear now, compared to eternal joy—" He smiled, lifting his hands and letting them fall open on his desk.

She drew in her breath and said carefully, "And when the world does not end on Saturday night, how will you deal with the damage you have caused?" He watched her, not answering, his expression settling back into that same faint contempt.

She stood, shoving back her chair noisily. "If you persist in this, it will be necessary to inform the authorities." She knew her threat sounded faintly silly, nor did he bother to ask her what authorities she had in mind. She waited an instant, but when he still didn't reply, she turned her back on him, intending to leave his office.

"Mrs. Park." His voice was loud, unexpectedly commanding, halting her in mid-step. "I see you are troubled," he said to her. She swung back to him, he was standing now, and he seemed somehow larger physically than she'd thought he was. Even as she opened her mouth to tell him this ploy was transparent and predictable, she became aware of the effort it had taken him to summon this sudden, surprising vitality, of how he had paused for the briefest instant, seeming to reach inside himself, and then, there it was. In spite of herself, she was impressed and also a little unnerved. "You feel yourself lost in a wilderness," he told her, his tone conversational. "And you are right. It is a wilderness." He paused. "Dangerous wild animals all around, the Native people of the forest, living so close to nature. And the snow. How it never stops." His tone had become lyrical, and he lifted a hand, palm open, as if it were snowing here in his office and he would catch and hold a glittering snowflake. She watched this performance, waiting for what would come next. "This is not the life you should be living," he said softly, and put out his hand to her, as if he would lead her to where she needed to go.

A rush of some powerful emotion had begun to move through her and she felt her face redden with it, a high, humming noise started in her ears. She didn't know what the emotion was, where it had come from, only that for an instant she had remembered Donald, remembered his very flesh, his voice, his scent. This was what she had not—no, never—allowed herself.

"Relief is so close," the pastor crooned. "Join us." She turned blindly from him and left his office and his church, pushing past Mrs. Vernon, who was in the narrow vestibule sweeping snow off her shabby boots.

She slipped and nearly fell hurrying down the bumpy, narrow path on her way out of the churchyard. The wind had risen and she lowered her head and pulled her wool scarf up around her cheeks and over her nose. She was angry with herself for letting the pastor upset her. This is how he keeps a congregation, she told herself. He finds the most desperate, he pretends to know things he can't possibly know, he deals in false mystery, he is a liar and a charlatan. But she had hurried past her own house and was at the end of the block before she realized it.

On Wednesday morning, with snow still pelting down, small dry pellets now that stung when the wind threw them against her face as she hurried to school, she went to the principal again.

"I think we should call an emergency meeting of parents to deal with this crisis." He'd been standing in the entrance watching the children tumble off the buses. He glanced at her quickly, frowning, then smoothed his face, moving closer to her.

"It's a tempest in a teapot," he said, his voice absurdly gentle, as if he were calming a child. "Monday morning it will all be over. Really, Astrid, trust me on this. It's best to just let it go." She realized with a shock that all his concern was for her.

She went back to her empty classroom—Wednesdays her children went first to Phys. Ed.—and sat at her desk, her head turned to where snow swept past the window in continuously dancing patterns of white on white. Watching it, bewildered, she asked herself, What have I been going through? What is the matter with me? As if Donald's death were no longer clear and simple, but had become some other, confusing thing. She sat, twisting her pen in her hands, watching the snow swirl and billow past the window, her mind circling around and around until she was roused by the return of her class.

She was wakened at midnight by the ringing of the phone and was up and hurrying to it, putting the receiver to her ear before she realized what she was doing. Again there was the loud hum, so that although she could hear the high-pitched murmur of a voice, the words were lost in the staticky drone. "Home?" was all she could make out, and then something that sounded like, "Donald." A shiver ran down her spine and she hunched her shoulders, grasping the phone in both hands.

"Leave me alone," she said. "Please, just leave me alone." The voice on the other end of the line was speaking again, sounding interrogatory now. "He is dead," she told it. "Donald is dead." Fumbling, she managed to hang up the phone. She wiped her face on her nightgown, although she hadn't been aware she'd begun to cry, had felt nothing, only this strange wetness on her cheeks, then returned to her bed where almost immediately she fell into a deep sleep.

She dreamt that Donald was driving their car, she saw the accident that would kill him coming, but he seemed not to hear her warning and wouldn't stop. He fell against the steering wheel, dead, but she was somehow out of the car and falling through an endlessly deep bank of frigid, blindingly white snow.

Thursday morning the radio warned of a record snowfall with no end in sight. The bus drivers had begun to complain about road conditions; the snowploughs couldn't keep up, a bus had gotten stuck and had to be pulled out by a tractor while the children sat shivering in it and then were late for school. The schoolyard was so snow-filled, no ploughs being available to clean it, that the younger children had to have recess in the auditorium, while the older children stayed in their classrooms, drinking Cokes and listening to rock music, or playing sports in the gym. At noon there was a rolling-around-on-the-floor fight between two grade six boys. The entire school was affected, Astrid thought, by the pastor's decree, and perhaps also the weather, and a palpable tension ran through the halls and classrooms.

When the last bell rang and the children were rushing out to get on their buses, Astrid went to the exit to make sure that all her pupils' jackets were securely fastened, their mitts on, their scarves snugly in place around their pensive and trusting little faces. The director of education was there in conversation with the bus drivers and the principal, and she listened unashamedly while she tended to her children.

"I've thought of closing the school tomorrow until this snow stops and the municipality gets caught up with the ploughing," the director was saying.

"That wind comes up tonight, that's it," a driver said. The others murmured agreement, shaking their heads worriedly. The director went on, "If it's still snowing in the morning, listen to your radios for the announcement." They went slowly out, leaving behind puddles of melting snow on the tile. "Don't take any chances now," the director called after them. "That's pretty valuable cargo you're carrying."

Back in her empty classroom, Astrid sat gazing out the wall of windows at the seemingly impenetrable sheet of falling snow.

"Mrs. Park." A woman of medium height, overweight, but in the strong-looking way of countrywomen, wearing a fur-trimmed parka, snowpants, and boots, stood in the doorway. "I'm Jody's mother," she said. Astrid rose and went toward her, extending her hand. The woman did not take it. "Jody says that you told her that we are wrong about Saturday."

"She was distraught—" Astrid began, but Mrs. Akinson interrupted.

"This is our belief," she said. "When you tell our children differently, you violate your role in our community. It had better not happen again."

"I repeat," Astrid said, feeling blood rushing to her face, "she is eight years old and she is terrified." Mrs. Akinson's calm— how surprisingly well spoken she was—helped Astrid to contain her emotion, but the woman was already turning away. "Wait," Astrid said. "The world is ending in two days and you take the time to come here and confront me? I think that is proof that you no more believe this ridiculous claim than I do." Then uncertainty struck her, the absurdity of the situation, the fear that she would now probably be fired for having interfered in community affairs and for quarrelling with a parent, and she put her hand up to her face.

"Your soul is in mortal jeopardy," Mrs. Akinson said, "and all you can think of is to attack us. I know your kind." She said it with such a cold firmness that Astrid, who felt she shouldn't be letting this ignorant woman insult her, was appalled to find that, instead of anger, what she felt was an overwhelming eagerness to be told, *Please, what kind am I?*

On Friday morning it was still snowing, although the dreaded wind had not come up. But fewer than half her children were present and none of those whose families belonged to the Church of Holy Brethren. She spent the morning reading stories to the few left and helping them paint pictures and do puzzles. At noon, Warren announced over the intercom that as the weather report wasn't good, the buses would be coming to take home those children whose parents weren't able to come for them. After they'd all gone, and most of the teachers too, Astrid tried to work at her desk, but she felt depressed and drained of energy and couldn't concentrate.

At home she tried to read a novel, but a restlessness had taken hold of her and she couldn't concentrate on it either and thought of going out. She wanted to pass by the church to see if anyone was there, and if there were, she imagined herself going inside and—doing what? Doing battle with the pastor in front of his parishioners? Of course not, she just wanted to be there to see what was happening, she told herself. But it worried her, too, that she was unable to dismiss the situation as everyone else did. For the first time she felt less sure that she was right and they were wrong. Anyway, the weather was too threatening now to go outside.

She was wakened in the night by the scream and thud of wind as it buffeted her house. Alarmed, she got up, noticing at once how very cold the house had grown, and pulled back the curtain at her bedroom window. She could see nothing but a torrent of white pelting furiously past the glass. When she clicked the lamp's switch, nothing happened. She was used to the power being interrupted as a result of a variety of weather conditions, and she merely left her freezing bedroom and retrieved from the porch the kerosene heater the owner of the house had left for such emergencies. She carried it into the living room, filled it from the five-gallon pail of kerosene she'd bought from him, and in a few minutes had it running. Then she went back to the bedroom, wrapped herself in her down-filled quilt, and returned to the living room, shutting the doors leading to the other rooms in order to conserve what little heat was left and that generated by the heater. The clock on her desk told her it was three in the morning.

She sat down in her one armchair, her feet off the cold floor on the footstool, pulled the quilt up around her, and tucked it around her feet, shoulders, and under her chin. The light from the heater cast glowing orange bars across the floor and she leaned back in her chair, watching them dance, and listening apprehensively to the wind on the roof, banging and tearing at the shingles. Its roar was so powerful she could almost believe it alive and a malevolent force out to destroy her house, the village, everyone in it. She was afraid, but she'd survived storms like this one the previous winter, she had shelter, she told herself, she would be all right, and the noise became, in a curious way, almost lulling, and she grew drowsy and soon slept.

She dreamt she was in the church with Pastor Vernon and his congregation. Candles burned at the end of every pew, dozens lit the altar, and torches hung at intervals down each side of the long, bare walls. There was an unrelenting noise, a high-pitched whine with a hint at back of it of something celestial—the singing of angels, perhaps. The pastor stood at the front of the church preaching. He was thin, almost skeletal, and his handsome face was oddly, startlingly paper-white as if he had already withdrawn to the next world and had sent back only his ghost. A woman screamed, a long high note, and fell forward over the pew in front of her, and a man stood, raising his arms to the ceiling and calling out in a voice that had a strange, non-human timbre and that rose to meld with the background wail. In the wide space between the pastor and the first row of pews lay a heap of children, their flaccid bodies piled crookedly on top of each other. Astrid saw clearly that their souls had departed. Then the church darkened ominously, the noise lifted to a deafening pitch and there was a loud crash.

She leaped from her chair, the quilt falling to the floor, and looked frantically around, remembering where she was and what was happening at the same time as she became aware of a freezing draft of wind and that the ill-fitting kitchen door was vibrating rapidly and noisily in its frame. And wasn't there a faint pealing in the background, as if the phone had been ringing all along? Trembling, she hurried to the door and pushed it open. Snow was piling up in the sink and spilling over onto the floor, and she realized that the crash she'd heard had been wind-hurled debris breaking her kitchen window. Snow-laden, icy wind swept in and she put up her hands to shield her face, edging first to the phone and lifting it to find that, of course, it was dead. Still fighting the last fragments of her dream, she understood, though, that she would have to block off the broken window or she really might freeze.

An old rag rug left by the owner lay in her tiny porch and, fear spurring her, she got it, rolled it into a ball, and shoved it into the snowy space left by the broken glass. Then she tacked up a blanket over the window with hands grown awkward and stiff with the cold. That done, she pushed the snow on the counter into the sink and added the snow from the floor to it.

Shaky from her scare, her exertions, and from the cold, she shut the kitchen door and hurried back to her chair. Glancing at the clock she was surprised to find that it was six in the morning, that she'd slept a couple of hours. Now she realized that the high-pitched scream in her dream had to have been the storm's howl, and she remembered dismally her dream-self that had wanted it to be a choir of angels.

She thought of the schoolchildren who would have had ample time to get home before the storm had broken, and were surely safe. Anybody who wasn't already in the church couldn't get there now, though, and she imagined the pastor waiting out the end of the world all by himself. It was a scene that saddened her, and she thought it a shame that a man of such unusual charisma had chosen to apply it in so fraudulent and ultimately useless a way. His character must somehow be deeply flawed, she mused: excessive vanity, or laziness, or some profound fear of living a real life in the real world like everyone else.

She thought, too, of Mrs. Akinson and wondered what

would make such a seemingly sensible person believe him, but found she couldn't understand the reasons, other than that of spiritual desperation, which she recognized as a cliché, and mistrusted as such. Maybe it's only that he catches people and holds onto them by sheer personal magnetism, not by wisdom or selflessness as true spiritual leaders do. A thief of souls, she thought, that's what he is. Then she shivered and began to tremble through her whole body, and couldn't stop for a long time, no matter how she snuggled into her quilt and pressed her back against the warmth of her chair.

She dreamt again unusually active, vivid dreams. In them she and Donald were meeting for the first time: he was smiling, then touching her forehead with his, so gently that she flushed with a heat both sexual and love-filled; they were at a party, he was telling a joke, then dancing with her; then they were in their own apartment eating breakfast at the small table in the kitchen. Donald seemed younger, softer than she remembered him being.

She woke a few hours later, looking around wonderingly, noticing that her heater had used up its fuel and gone out and that the room was so cold she could see her breath. She knew at once by the stillness that the storm was over, and then realized that someone was pounding on her door. Clutching her quilt around her shoulders, she went slowly to it and pushed it open. Sunlight striking the wind-sculptured banks and sheets of snow flooded in, so bright that she had to put a hand over her eyes, but the blessed post-storm peace and the wonder that always accompanied it touched her too, and she hesitated an instant before she backed away into the room's relative darkness.

"You look all right," a man boomed at her in that hearty way all the men here adopted for social exchanges. She recognized the district's robust young reeve by his voice, and lowered her arm from her face, hearing the faint roar of a snowplough somewhere out in the village. "Power company says it'll be at least tomorrow before the electricity comes on again. Storm took down a hundred poles and lines are down all over the place." Before she could answer, he went on. "The dance hall's got backup propane heat and we're taking all you ladies over there." He added quickly, "Need somebody able-bodied like you to make coffee and sandwiches for the boys on the ploughs." Knowing she had no choice, she went to dress. Outside in the blazing light, male voices were shouting across the banks of snow, and behind them she heard the whine of motors she took to be snowmobiles.

"Men just love a good disaster," one of the old ladies in the hall said to her, her dark eyes alight with humour and intelligence. The village's handful of old women were wrapped in blankets and seated in comfortable chairs while they waited for the roads to open so their relatives could come for them. Children played board games at the tables, or ran about giggling and dodging each other, and the murmur of women's voices came from the kitchen. At the far end of the hall a few men were setting up the last of the long wooden tables and placing wooden stacking chairs around them. Astrid suddenly realized that one of the men was Pastor Vernon, that the other men working with him, the children, and also the women in the kitchen must be his flock rescued from the church. Pastor Vernon lifted his head from his task; his eyes met hers, giving no glint of recognition; he went back to his work as if he hadn't seen her. Steeling herself, Astrid went to the kitchen and pushed open the door.

For an instant every eye in the room was on her, a hush fell; just as suddenly the glances dropped, the women went back to the buttering of bread, to the rattling of plates and cups. She recognized the pastor's wife and, across the central worktable facing her, Jody Akinson's mother. That she'd been the object of censuring conversation among them was obvious. She felt her face growing hot and, without speaking, backed hastily out of the room, deciding that she would instead help by entertaining the children and chatting with the old people.

Astrid had been reading a story to three little girls at the end of a long table when one of the mothers came to take them to their makeshift beds on the stage. She watched them go, then continued her gaze around the hall, lit, now that evening had come, by a variety of kerosene and battery-powered camping lamps which, turned low so the children and old people might sleep, cast a comforting yellow-orange light edged by shadows. The women murmured softly to their children or each other, the men, exhausted from their long shifts in the snow and cold, dozed in chairs or stretched out on the floor, or sat playing cards at a table by the kitchen. She watched the pastor pacing alone with his Bible at the hall's far end. A chair scraped the floor and she turned to it to find Mrs. Akinson sitting down across from her.

After a moment Astrid asked, "Is tonight ..." Mrs. Akinson said, glancing down the hall toward him, "The pastor says he believes he misunderstood when he was in prayer, that he had the wrong date. It isn't tonight." She spoke quietly, but Astrid could feel a sadness wafting from her, or perhaps it was merely weariness, the same bone-deep weariness she felt herself.

"You mean," she said, as the message with its implication of other dates began to sink in, "that you will go through *this* again and again?" She couldn't keep the distaste out of her voice. Colour flooded Mrs. Akinson's neck, then her cheeks and her forehead. She stared at Astrid, a depth appearing in her eyes, as if this meaning were just dawning on her, too.

"I think—" she began, then stopped, her face working as she struggled to maintain her composure.

Astrid leaned toward her. *"Death is not so cheap,"* she said. *"I have suffered a great loss, and I can tell you that, for people like us"*—she glanced around the hall, meaning more than these few people, but the dead in wars, of starvation, and disease all around the world—"I can tell you that *death* is not so easy. You have children—your *children*—" She shook her head, then sat back in her chair, staring at Mrs. Akinson.

The pastor's voice suddenly rose out of the background murmur, his words not quite distinguishable, and both of them turned to glance at the far end of the hall where he was engaged in an intense conversation, perhaps even an argument, with some of his male parishioners. Embarrassed, the two women turned back to each other.

"We would all have died to eternal life," Mrs. Akinson whispered to Astrid, much as the children in Astrid's class would give a memorized answer that they didn't understand, but knew was the right one, to a question she'd asked. Astrid didn't reply, distracted as she was by some other emotion that was struggling to free itself. She wasn't sure what it was, and would have gotten up now and gone away, except that suddenly she found herself too tired to move. She began to wish she had not been so hard on Mrs. Akinson who, despite her denial, she could see now, had suffered. I have been suffering too, she thought, but the worst is over now.

She found herself edging out her hand across the table until her fingers grazed Mrs. Akinson's. Mrs. Akinson did not draw back her hand, but left it there, and they sat that way for a long time, in silence, never looking at each other, their fingers touching.

Saskatchewan

She doubts it's a good title, imagines it in the ironic, wavering type of *The New Yorker* and then in the sterner, more assertive type of *Saturday Night*, and would go further, but her memory for the handful of top-flight magazines and their typefaces fails her. And anyway, marvel of marvels, they have once again achieved flight; below them Saskatchewan is at once shrinking and expanding as they rise.

She wonders what picture the word *Saskatchewan* might evoke in readers of *The New Yorker*, thinks hopefully: a wild, rugged country of raging rivers, impenetrable black forests, jagged snow-covered mountains, and canoes full of Indians. As it appeared, in fact, in that old bomb of a movie, *Saskatchewan*, with Alan Ladd and Shelley Winters, filmed, in fact, in Alberta. She knows a reader of *Saturday Night* would see a sort of impossibly extended, frozen dogpatch. But what does the word conjure for her, who has spent her life in Saskatchewan? It stretches below her, unfortunately flat all around its capital and, to complete the stereotype, newly snow-covered. She closes her eyes, mouths "Saskatchewan," and swirling snow scuds across a field of wind-packed, glossy ice. Nothing moves, even the few bare trees look as if they're about to shatter with cold. She sighs and opens her eyes.

It's her familiar defensiveness, she knows it, taking hold as she flies off to the dreaded East. Maybe she should call the story she's working on "Toronto," she thinks, since so much of what she does is defined by the place, though she's been there for maybe a total of two weeks in her life and knows nobody. Or almost nobody. She has one friend, Hannah, with whom she'll be staying.

The man sitting beside her is studying the interior of his briefcase, a shabby leather satchel of the kind male students used to carry when she was still a city girl, and in university thirty years earlier. Therefore not a businessman, probably a professor. He has a pleasant face, dark wavy hair, long and unfashionable.

The flight attendant offers drinks which Jenna refuses. Her seatmate orders whisky, and catching its scent, her mouth waters. But no, she can't tackle the Toronto airport drunk, she'd never be heard from again. Before she can stop herself she's made a disparaging snort out loud. She should wear a sign: *I am alone too much. I talk to myself.*

He turns out to be a composer. This is so surprising after years of sitting beside businessmen who ignore her or give her unasked-for paternal advice about flights and hotels that she's silenced. When she tells him her name and that she's a writer, and the name of her just-released, latest novel, she sees that neither means anything to him. Although she reminds herself that she's never heard of him either, this still depresses her and she thinks woefully, as if she's thinking about a good friend, of the ambition with which she feels herself saddled, a burden she has wearily to carry, barely manages to keep at a socially acceptable level.

And, once they start talking about the arts, she discovers

glumly she doesn't know any of the well-known writers who are apparently acquaintances of his. It's because she doesn't live in a city, doesn't even live near one, and knows, too, that this is viewed as a personal failing by the people she has to deal with in cities, an inexplicable character flaw for which she'd be forgiven if she lived on a chic acreage on a city's outskirts and had an artist husband. She imagines a sculptor working in iron high up a ladder, his head vanished inside a welder's helmet, his torch hissing, then a potter squatting in front of the barn at a raku fire.

But she lives on a real working ranch, has a real cowboy for a husband who comes in with manure on his boots and hay stuck in his clothes and who, preoccupied with his own world, is rarely more than mildly curious about hers. People don't ask about him, she doesn't know why not, unless the apparent sheer improbability of their mating boggles them too much.

Jenna and the composer settle into a camaraderie based on the fact that they're both artists. He lives in Victoria but he's crossing the country to sit on an arts jury about which he's discreetly silent. Jenna knows it's bad form to talk about it, as she's still suffering from the repercussions of sitting on a jury that gave the country's top literary prize to the wrong person. She's glad not to talk about it, tries not even to think about it.

They share a small bottle of wine, exchange addresses and phone numbers, though Jenna doubts they'll ever meet again, and finally, after seeing the mass of people vying for taxis, share one downtown from the mouth of hell, otherwise known as the Toronto airport.

It's raining gently when she says goodbye to the composer, gets out of the cab in front of a big brick house near Bloor Street, and takes her bag. As the taxi swishes away on the wet pavement, she pauses, lifts her face to the rain-dampened branches of the old trees that line Hannah's street, and feels its soft patting on her face. How easily it rains here, she thinks, as if rain were nothing at all. The glimpses of sky she sees between the branches are luminescent but starless, the city itself glows, a star fallen to earth. She climbs the wooden steps, crosses the decaying porch, and before she can knock, Hannah appears in the square of light, holding the door open for her.

Although their friendship dates back to university days, they never talk about when they were students together in faraway Saskatoon, part of a group of women grad students whose allegiance to each other cut across colleges and departments, and survived through divorces, affairs, depressions, and heartbreak. Curled up on the sofa while Hannah's cats walk across her lap, Jenna thinks how everything seemed to be falling apart in those days, hanging on was the best you could hope for, and she didn't even manage that, got married instead and went off, while Hannah stayed until she had a doctorate, an achievement of which Jenna is in awe.

"I saw your name in the paper," Hannah says. "Quite a few times, actually. It wasn't all flattering." Jenna can't think of any reason for her name to have been in the paper. "About the Bella Griffin thing," Hannah tells her, looking a little surprised. Bella Griffin is one of the country's best-known, bestselling authors. Jenna moans and puts her face in her hands.

"This upsets you," Hannah comments, an insight worthy of a doctor of psychology. For a second Jenna can't believe Hannah doesn't know anything about this. But then Hannah lives in a world of psychotherapy that Jenna finds mysterious and amazing: Adlerians, Jungians, Reichians—nobody in Hannah's world seems to be a Freudian—psychotherapists who drum, who use hypnosis, Hannah herself is an expert on the tarot. Jenna begins to explain, and the story floods out of her, unstoppable.

The truth is, she'd been surprised to have been asked to sit on the jury, assuming that as no readers seemed to have heard of her, neither had anybody else, including the arts organiza- tion awarding the prize, and so she agreed out of the fear that if she didn't, she'd instantly be erased from the history into which she'd so suddenly been written. She and the two other jurors spent hours locked together in a hotel room arguing politely—"Not all juries are so polite," the arts organization's officer said—and in Jenna's opinion, through the course of the long session, each juror demonstrated admirable integrity combined with a deep streak of perversity. She doesn't exclude herself from this analysis, and wonders if she'd been like the others, male and professors, whether their decision would have been the same. She knows she knuckled under, there's no other way to put it, and she pictures herself sinking to her knees as her legs turn to a pale, flesh-coloured water that soaks into the smart hotel rug.

Or maybe she didn't knuckle under. Maybe there was noth- ing she could have done to change the outcome short of forcing a hung jury. That would have created a huge scandal. But, in the end, a scandal was created anyway. Once their decision was known, critics surfaced across the country, although ninety per cent of them were in Toronto. They chastised the jury from television sets, radios, and newspapers with varying degrees of outrage for not choosing, in Jenna's opinion too, the wonderful fifteenth novel of Bella Griffin, which, if it hadn't exactly been a bestseller before the decision, certainly has been since.

"The other jurors must have had good reasons for choosing the book they did," Hannah points out in a reasonable, thera- pist's tone. Jenna considers. In fact, there'd been little discus- sion, she'd been unconvinced by anything they'd said, but their tones—full of certainty, expecting no disagreement—had quite simply scared her into silence.

"Who was I to argue with them?" she asks Hannah. "They

seemed so sure. I thought they knew better than I did." Hannah studies her, as if she sees something in her old friend's face that surprises and puzzles her. Jenna drops her eyes.

Though Hannah's sofa is wide and soft, Jenna spends most of the night tossing. All the city noises, that sense of it as a great beast curled up for the night, its breathing audible through the open window, keeps her awake. Toward morning she falls asleep and dreams she's strolling with her mother arm in arm down a city sidewalk. She and her mother got along badly, but ever since her mother's death at seventy-two, a few years earlier, she keeps appearing in Jenna's dreams, gentle and helpful, offering advice, opening her arms to Jenna as she never did in life. Strangely, Jenna never wakes bitter from one of these dreams, but instead, a little shaky and softened, as though a crusted and aching wound had been cleansed.

In the morning Hannah and Jenna drink coffee together before Hannah leaves for her office and Jenna sets out on the first day of her three-day visit to Toronto. Her new novel just out, this morning she'll be stopping in at her publisher's office to say hello and collect any advance reviews. Her publisher, a well-known, although small, company, occupies a set of tiny, crowded rooms in a dilapidated building just beyond the borders of the real downtown. Jenna decides that instead of pacing Hannah's apartment until it's time to take the subway, she'll walk to her meeting. She's not excited about it, she knows that a staffer half her own age will greet her, that probably she'll be taken by this young woman to lunch somewhere, where they'll have a hard time making conversation, and the next time Jenna meets her—if she does—she won't even recognize the girl.

Still, it's a warm, early fall day and the walk is interesting. It feels good to be marching down a city sidewalk again, her hands in her pockets, as if she belongs here. At moments like this, when she's alone in the city, some knotted place inside her loosens and relaxes. Nearly thirty years in the country and when she's not angry with the city, or out of her depths, her youthful days in one return to her and she feels happy and at home.

This afternoon she's to do an interview at an ethnic radio station and two more at strange little magazines, places so obscure that she's never heard of them, and knows she herself will never see or hear the interviews. Then, tomorrow night, she'll give a reading at a downtown library. It's the first time she's been invited to read in Toronto, and she alternates between excitement about it and a darker mood that eventually overtakes her every time she comes here. She suspects if she could isolate its cause it wouldn't do her credit. It's a deep-rooted anger, she thinks, a helpless, smouldering rage that this is the wall she has to scale—big-city indifference, big-city arrogance.

And yet, in her country home she's still seen as the city woman—never will be anything else—while here she's classified as purely country. Worst of all, she can't tell herself any more which is closest to the truth.

Once, when she'd stumbled on a psychic fair by accident, she'd paid twenty dollars to have an earnest young clairvoyant mistake this thing that drives her for alcoholism. The comparison is too apt to be funny. Yes, she's addicted, she's out of control. And she refuses, except in moments of despair, to attribute her lack of success to her shortcomings as a writer. She knows this is blindness, something with which she still has to come to terms. But she's far from ready to accept she may not be as good as she thinks she is—she's published, isn't she? Never has any trouble finding a publisher, her reviews are good. She jerks her mind away, tries to pay attention to the people she's meeting as she walks along the busy sidewalk toward her publisher's.

•   •   •

The day having gone pleasantly, if dully, and it being the day Hannah teaches a night class at the university, Jenna decides to spend the evening at a movie. Since her departure to the ranch she's had to give up movies—the nearest movie theatre is fifty miles away, and tends, anyway, to show only Hollywood spectaculars. Now, whenever she's in a city, she tries to see at least one. She often thinks she shouldn't, because one movie is never enough to satisfy, yet more would move her into some other, almost-forgotten realm from which she'd only have to return the moment she got on the plane that would take her home. But lately, oddly, her desire for even one movie has been failing her, as if her last hold on her former city-self is disintegrating. About this, she alternates between being discomfited and relieved.

At ten o'clock, in the warm fall darkness, Jenna starts the walk back to Hannah's apartment. She sees the Brunswick Avenue sign, recognizes the street as literary in some way she can't remember, and decides to walk down it. Leaves from the big maples that line the avenue coat the sidewalk and in the light from the street lamps Jenna sees they're the big, three-pointed ones in vivid reds that are on the Canadian flag.

She slows to a stroll and studies the old brick houses. Some have ornate, wrought-iron fences separating the small squares of grass from the sidewalk and most have stained-glass sections in their front door, or flanking them. The interior lights make the colours glow. How beautiful these houses must once have been, she thinks, for now they have a shabby air, they're on their last legs. Once they must have been the homes of the bourgeoisie, surely working-class people couldn't have afforded them. But she has little experience of the bourgeoisie, the only members of it she's ever met were the failures, the black sheep, the kids who'd been sent to her high school where the poor kids went, after they'd been expelled from all the others. She remembers them as nice kids, but so frozen in their misery and frightened by finding themselves there that they never made any friends at all, and not one of them lasted a full school year. And there is no bourgeoisie in the part of Saskatchewan where Jenna lives. Just farmers and ranchers with their own hidden and tense pecking order she only, after about twenty years, began to decipher, but the nuances of which still sometimes elude her, so that she has to ask her husband to explain a fleeting expression or an apparently offhand remark that everybody else seems to understand.

A woman's voice floats out from the shadows across the street. She's singing in a breathy contralto, wobbling on the sustained notes, a little off-pitch, an old song about September. Jenna holds her breath. The warmth, the intimacy of the voice, suffused as it is with longing, weaving through the leafy darkness, turns the street into a boudoir. A shiver runs down her back and she slows even more, trying to see the singer, or discover which embowered porch she's singing from, but the night and the trees hide her.

Hannah is sipping a glass of wine and laying out a tarot deck on the coffee table when Jenna lets herself in.

"It's one of the new decks I bought in New York," she tells her as Jenna pours herself wine and stretches out on the sofa. "I'm trying to learn it." Hannah owns dozens of decks, forever picking up new ones as they're developed. It fascinates Jenna that Hannah finds the tarot at least as useful as Freud or Jung. Jenna herself relies for advice on the *I Ching*. "The Wanderer," she keeps drawing. *Strange lands and separation are the wanderer's lot.* She wonders if she should regard this as a directive or not, for although she has no plans to leave her husband and the ranch, neither has she been able to fully imagine living there until she dies. Whenever she tries, the future soon fades into a tangle of contradictory pictures and ideas, and Jenna draws back in perplexity.

Hannah says, "I read that interview with Bella Griffin in the paper. She's caustic."

"Vitriolic," Jenna agrees. "Have you read any of her books?" Expressionless, Hannah reaches to the floor beside her and holds up a copy of the book in question.

"Bought it today," she says, and breaks into a grin.

Jenna had flown home the day after the jury made its decision, and in the return to ranch life, though the decision dismayed her, she let it slip to the back of her mind. But as soon as the short list was released, the phone began to ring. Arts reporters from Toronto wanted to know what happened, why was Griffin ignored? She couldn't turn on the radio or TV without having to listen to panelists discussing the jury's decision in amazed and disapproving tones. The frustration of not being able to respond was such that finally, when she heard a censorious panel on the radio, she had to lie down with a fever. But she continued to believe Griffin's book to be the best and didn't know how to reply when she received a couple of letters commending the jury's decision.

At first Griffin said nothing about being left off the list, which Jenna regarded as proper and dignified, but eventually reports of her remarks about the verdict, which seemed to Jenna to ring with an unbecoming immodesty, reached her, and at last she began to be angry both at Griffin's refusal to accept the judgement and at finding herself in the impossible situation of having to remain silent about a decision with which she doesn't agree. But it's a sort of woeful, frustrated anger.

And when she thinks about what she knows of Griffin, that the woman would care at all surprises Jenna. It's not only that she's already won the prize twice, as well as other much-coveted prizes that Jenna never expects to see—at least, not for years and years—but that by all reports she's lived the most glamorous of lives, in the great cities of the world, knows the most famous writers, and has rich and powerful friends. She wonders if the two other men on the jury who wouldn't hear of giving the prize to Bella were merely jealous of her. The thought has crossed her mind before, but always she's dismissed it as mean-spirited.

She spends another restless night on Hannah's sofa. When she finally falls asleep, she dreams about her husband. He's riding in a wild, untamed country full of deep, crumbling coulees whose sides are studded with sage and cactus. He rides down their sides with fearless abandon, on a perfect forty-five-degree angle, away from her. He seems to be fused to his horse, as if they're one animal. When she wakes, she recognizes the dream as about the Archer, whose precise angle of travel represents the perfection of his fit to nature, and for a second she longs to be home.

This morning another junior staffer is going to take her around to bookstores so that she can sign stock. Jenna dreads this. Usually the bookstore staff doesn't recognize her name, which humiliates her, although she always pretends to find it amusing, and she's dismayed whether her books are on the shelves or not. If they're there, she thinks it's because nobody wants them, but if they're not, she thinks the same thing. She knows she's being ridiculous. It's her pride, it stems from her thwarted ambition that gnaws at her, and she can't tell if it's thwarted because she's unlucky or because she's a bad writer who merely thinks she's a good one.

Besides, she thinks, brightening, it's fun to walk or drive around the city with someone who knows her way, and at the end of the bookstore circuit, no matter how demoralizing, there will be another pleasant lunch in a nice restaurant. In the afternoon, she thinks, I'll go to the museum. And tonight is her reading, although she'll be only one of three readers. She wonders if she'll be allotted the prestigious last position, or if, ignominiously, she'll be assigned to read first.

The day unfolds predictably, and when evening comes, Hannah accompanies her to the library, then seats herself in the small auditorium among the audience of fifty or so people. The young publicist, Carol, with whom Jenna spent the morning doing the bookstore circuit, arrives and sits beside Hannah, while Jenna is introduced by a librarian to the other readers, both younger than she is. The woman, having just published her first short-story collection to excellent reviews, is giddy with excitement, and when asked to read first, doesn't appear to mind. Jenna suspects she doesn't yet know what this means. The man, grungy in torn jeans and faded T-shirt, his hair uncombed and his attitude, at best, impassive, is a prize-winning Toronto poet. The minute she hears his name she knows *he'll* be the one to read last.

Although she dreams of the day when she'll be the only one on the program, tonight she finds she's relieved to read with others, especially local writers who will draw an audience she knows that in this city she'd never get on her own. Although she hopes—no, she tells herself, she believes—she's past the day when only one person, or no one at all, will show up at her reading.

Happily, the young woman, Gillian, doesn't read too long, and both funny and charming—Jenna sees that one day she may also be a very good writer—she leaves the audience in a receptive mood for Jenna's turn. Jenna has chosen the section she'll read with care; she wants these listeners to see that she isn't mediocre, that she's much better than Gillian who now sits smiling up at Jenna with glittering eyes and flushed cheeks, obviously not hearing a word Jenna reads. Jenna wants to hold her listeners' attention so that while she is reading they can't look away or move; she wants each of her words to fall on them like single stones tossed into water. She isn't a bit nervous—at moments like this, something deep inside her, for which she has no name, no explanation, grips her and carries her through.

When she has finished, to brief but, she thinks hopefully, enthusiastic applause, there's an intermission. Then it's the poet's turn. He goes on for more than half an hour, until people begin to get up and sidle out quietly. He doesn't look up from his page, he mumbles something between poems now and then, but if his remarks are complete sentences, Jenna can't figure them out. It amazes her that any writer could be so cavalier about an audience. Unless that's his point, she thinks. But then, why come at all?

Finally, it's over. Jenna is about to suggest to Hannah that they stop somewhere on the way home for a drink, when Hannah yawns and says, "Well, let's go, I have to be up early tomorrow." Disappointed, Jenna reaches to take her coat from Carol.

"I have to drop over to the launch for Eric Anderson's new book. Would you mind coming with me?" Carol asks. Eric Anderson is literary star, one of the biggest, another one Jenna's never met or even, come to think of it, seen in the flesh.

Hannah says, "Go, Jen, I'll take a cab home. You'll have fun." She turns away, waving at Jenna over her shoulder.

"It's good for you to be seen around, " Carol tells her seriously. Jenna can't figure out if Carol just doesn't want to go alone, or if some senior person at the publishing house has told Carol to take Jenna out after her reading. She hesitates, then decides that it doesn't matter what Carol's reason is, and agrees to go.

She and Carol go out of the library and Carol flags down a cab. They get in and in moments they've arrived in the middle of a series of old stone buildings which Jenna recognizes, even in the shadowy darkness, are on the university campus. Carol and the cab driver confer and soon he pulls up to a side door of a rust-coloured stone building.

As the cab drives away from the leaf-littered curb, Carol pushes open the heavy oak door, they enter a hallway, and then go through open double doors leading into a large, dark room, an auditorium, full of people, all standing and looking toward a low stage in the far corner where someone Jenna can't see is making a speech. It must be witty because every once in a while the people around Jenna break into laughter. She tries to hear what the speaker is saying, but in the crush, and the near-darkness and her unfamiliarity with the situation, she can't get the words to make any sense.

The man on the stage has been replaced by a woman who is introducing someone else. As the crowd claps for the new speaker, Jenna stops where she is and joins in, then, because she can't see the stage at all from where she is now, keeps moving, making her way out of the crush of people toward a wall she can lean against. Finally, she reaches a stretch of wall, but here it is all occupied, and so, fearful of attracting attention to herself, she keeps walking slowly along the outer edge of the crowd. At last, on the side of the hall away from the stage, she sees a place to stand, and squeezing past people, moves toward it.

She's nearly there when a tall, slender woman abruptly turns directly into Jenna's path and they nearly collide. It takes her an instant, during which she's apologizing, to realize she's face to face with Bella Griffin. Griffin appears as startled by Jenna as Jenna is by her.

"Ahh," Bella says. "I think I know you—you're Jenna Messer." Jenna is too flustered now to say anything. It's hard to see in the dim light, but Jenna thinks Bella's expression is disapproving, and she has to subdue the urge to say, "Excuse me," and to dive back into the thickest part of the crowd. There is a long silence which Jenna is too nervous to break and which Bella seems disinclined to do. She observes that this woman is old, seventy if she's a day, and she realizes she's always thought of Bella Griffin as having stopped aging at about sixty.

"I seem to have lost track of the people I came with," Jenna says irrelevantly. "I mean, uh—I'm very glad to meet you." Bella is holding a wineglass and Jenna realizes now that everybody has one and that somewhere in this huge room there must be a bar and a table of snacks. Bella hasn't made any move to give Jenna her hand, and confused, Jenna is about to speak again when Bella says firmly, "Let's talk," as if she's just made a decision about something. "There's a lounge over there." She turns peremptorily and strides away, not even glancing back to see if Jenna is behind her. Meekly, Jenna follows. Her mouth has gone dry, and she wishes she had a glass of wine, is immediately glad she doesn't, because then she'd only say stupid things.

On her right, through a break in the crowd, she sees Carol in earnest conversation with a group of young women, all rail-thin and dressed alike in flat shoes, tights, very short skirts, and sweaters that hug their tiny breasts and concave midriffs. She thinks how they all look to her like they bathe too much, and is appalled that in such a moment she can still have these ridiculous but, nonetheless, interesting thoughts.

They enter the lounge, it's empty, they must have all gone to hear the speeches, and Jenna sees the bar across the room. Bella goes straight to a corner and sits down on a narrow, L-shaped sofa, and waits for Jenna. Obediently, Jenna sits kitty-corner to her. The lights in this room haven't been dimmed, and when she glances at Bella, Jenna sees that although she was once a beauty, her skin has that powdery look of the aged, and is criss-crossed with a pattern of tiny wrinkles. But her eyes are as sharp and bright as a child's, although without the child's quality of eager innocence.

"Are you enjoying your stay in the city?" Bella asks her politely. Jenna hesitates, then says, "I find it interesting—this event, for instance." She looks back through the open door to the darkened room beyond. She suppresses the urge to chatter on about how she got here by accident, has never attended an event quite like this one. "I enjoyed your last novel very much," she says, then immediately thinks, Oh, God, why did I say that—she won't believe me.

"Thank you," Bella says. "I'm afraid I haven't read any of your books." Jenna says nothing. There's a sudden burst of laughter from the auditorium and Jenna gives an involuntary start.

"You're not used to crowds," Bella says. "It is very crowded in there."

"Country dances used to be much more packed than that," Jenna says. "And noisier. But all that has passed ..." She can hardly launch into an explanation about rural depopulation, and lets her voice trail away. Bella is scrutinizing her with her penetrating grey-green eyes, as if she would see exactly what makes Jenna tick.

Under her silent gaze Jenna's sense of irony, which she wears as armour in the city to protect her from all the things she doesn't understand, isn't part of, that she at once longs for and hates, slowly deserts her. For an instant, in its place panic threatens, and then recedes. She flounders, confused and not knowing what to think or say, feeling her face growing hot, and her hands perspiring like a grubby child's. In the face of Bella's polish and sophistication, she sees herself as a forty-eight-year-old woman who doesn't pay enough attention to her hair and nails, or to fashion and diet, to undergarments or shoes, sitting in the midst of an event to which everybody who is anybody has come—only she doesn't know who everybody is, nor anybody—and she's suddenly very tired.

Bella says, "A long time ago I came from the country too." She looks down at her long-fingered, elegantly groomed hands. "When I was young I went to France to become a painter. At an embassy reception for Canadian artists, I met my husband." Jenna nods, but Bella isn't looking at her. "I've written in cities on three or four continents over the years," she continues. "I wrote, and lived, in the tradition that a writer was someone who was familiar with the wider world."

"Yes?" Jenna says, suspecting she's being insulted, and trying to sound cold, but succeeding only in sounding querulous. Bella glances at her and then looks down to her hands again, smoothing one with the other so that slender mauve veins rise.

"Such a long time ago," she says, as if she's a little embarrassed by having spoken so much.

Jenna says matter-of-factly, "I've lived thirty years in the country. When I married my husband I wasn't writing, hadn't thought of such a thing. I didn't make my choice with that kind of future in mind." She lifts her head and meets Bella's gaze full on, but Bella lowers her eyes quickly, as if she doesn't want Jenna to guess what she's thinking. Jenna's tiredness feels huge to her, but she's beginning to recognize what it is. She struggles against it, but it's no use. "I think—" she begins, then stops. Bella waits, not lifting her head. "The truth is," Jenna tells her, "that, for me, there was no choice. Your book was head and shoulders better than the others." She half expected she would have to explain to Bella what she's referring to, but Bella lifts her head instantly to fasten her gaze on Jenna.

"Am I to believe that?" she asks sharply.

"Yes," Jenna says. There is a long silence, Bella's patrician expression wavering and then quickly returning.

"Tell me, then," she says slowly, "what were the objections

of the others?" Jenna hesitates. "Oh, yes," she says angrily. "You're not supposed to tell me."

"I can't remember," Jenna says too quickly. One of them had said, "It's just Bella doing what she always does," in a bored, dismissive tone. Jenna doesn't repeat this. "They just weren't interested, I guess."

"And you couldn't persuade them otherwise, I take it," Bella says, and laughs lightly, as if she's afraid she's revealed too much with this remark. Jenna winces and lowers her eyes. What she was going to say to excuse herself was that she wasn't used to such occasions, she wasn't used to having power, the city frightened her—but with Bella Griffin right here in front of her, waiting for an explanation, she sees the futility, even the insult, of offering this.

She's shocked at herself, her cheeks are heating again with something like shame. She says, "I am to blame. I thought—I was afraid," she says. "I was afraid because—" She stops. The air in the room is still, but it seems to Jenna that it has gained texture, that it waits for her, too, as Bella is doing. There's another burst of noise from the outer room, clapping, then loud conversation, laughter, the sound of people milling about. Now some are drifting slowly into the lounge.

"There's no excuse," she says, and meets Bella's eyes. "I've blamed them as jealous, as men—older men—assuming their right to make the decision and ignoring my opinion as value-less. The jury officer even told me to argue with them and I said, 'What can I say to these men?' and both men dropped their eyes and fiddled with their papers. I could have swayed them then, if I'd tried. I *could* have—but I didn't. I—it was—I know what it was." She's afraid she's going to cry, and furious with herself, blinks rapidly until the urge vanishes.

Bella looks as if she's about to speak, but Jenna lifts a hand to stop her. Even as she does it, she finds herself smiling at the preposterous imperiousness of her gesture. More people are moving into the lounge now, heading for the bar or to the table of snacks. She leans closer to Bella to be heard over their chatter and says quickly, "It was that I couldn't part with what I knew. What I knew about books, I mean, about writing them. I was biding my time; it seemed too soon." Bella is perfectly still, listening with her whole body. "I gave no thought to you," Jenna confesses. "It *was* my fault."

She had said, of the book they'd chosen, "It never sang for me," and that had made the men glance quickly at each other, and then down, shuffling their papers again. She doesn't know why she'd said that, when she might have said other, more discerning things. And she doesn't know what the men—university professors both—were thinking of when they'd acted as if she'd embarrassed them: that she was stupid and wrong? That she was right? That they didn't understand what it meant to have a book sing for you as Bella's had done?

Bella doesn't move. She is staring down at her hands, tightly clasped now and resting on her lap, as if she's weighing what Jenna has just said. Jenna waits, breathless, for whatever wisdom—or anger—Bella might choose to impart to her. Waiting, her heart beating too fast, she becomes aware that someone is standing nearby. She glances up and sees a young, handsome man in a dark suit, neat shirt and tie, and polished black, tasselled loafers. He's staring with an eager smile at Bella, as if he knows her and is just waiting for her to notice him.

He says, "Miss Griffin, we've met? I'm ...." Jenna stops listening. To her surprise, Bella smiles graciously at him, if distantly, and murmurs something that is clearly permission for him to go on talking to her. Jenna waits, expecting Bella to turn back to her, perhaps to introduce the young man.

But Bella doesn't, it's as if Jenna has become invisible, and after a moment, Jenna realizes she's been dismissed, that to stay on would only invite further insult. Or at least that's what she's thinking, as she rises awkwardly and walks slowly away toward Carol, who is standing in the doorway across the room, evidently waiting for her. She's ready to turn back should Bella call her name, but this doesn't happen.

The next morning, after kissing Hannah goodbye, she takes a cab to the airport an hour before she needs to. Now all she wants to do is get out of this city. But as soon as she makes her way onto her plane and settles into her seat she feels her spirits plummeting back into that mood the city always induces. She's brooding, morose, sullen; she is, she thinks ironically, completely herself again.

As the plane lifts off the runway she finds herself wondering if she'd told Bella the truth, and if she hadn't, as she suspects, what the truth might be. She thinks, I am simply a coward, afraid to speak up against two men; she thinks, I don't know enough about literature to be on a jury. She knows that she has far too much pride to admit either of these—whether true or not—to anyone. Anyway, she tells herself, it's worse than that. Surprised at herself, she struggles to put into words this amorphous sense of guilt and shame that she feels, that nothing she's so far thought of has managed to dispel.

Although it was raining and foggy when they left Toronto, here, high above the Manitoba-Saskatchewan border, they're flying in pale fall sunshine. Below them the Great Plains glisten white, and then, as the sun sinks and they approach Regina, they glow a deep, resonant blue. She is coming home again, to the place where she was born, with its miles of open, grassy plains, its fields of crops, its thick northern forests, its multitude of lakes and rivers, even its sand dunes, river rapids, and its waterfalls.

Gazing down, she thinks, I know its secrets, I know what

matters about this place, I know what it *is*—or, at least, I can keep searching for that, I can keep trying to say it—

To take responsibility for what I know, she thinks, that's what I haven't wanted to do. And she realizes that when she denied Bella Griffin, she also denied herself. It seems to her that at some level she's always known this, and has refused it, craving instead a world she can't have. But now they're rushing downward for a landing, the plane quivering and whining against the air's resistance, the its power pushing her back against her seat. As they plunge downward through layers of resonant blue toward the vast, mysterious plains below, she feels an unexpected answering surge of emotion, visceral and powerful, and after a second, she recognizes it as the purest joy.

Gravity

Louisa has been thinking about Pat, and the girl's face had intruded again, her stillness, so that when Nick rides up to her and bends down from his horse to speak to her where she's leaning against the truck's grill, she nearly jumps out of her skin. "We'll stop up at the corner for lunch," he says. "They're played out from that uphill climb."

"Okay," she says, as if they haven't been stopping for lunch at this rare patch of unploughed and unfenced grass every year for the last twenty. He rides off again to join the others, and she gets back into the driver's seat, starts the half-ton, and moves it slowly ahead.

At the top of a long hill that leads down past stubble fields on both sides of the road, with miles of grassed and rolling ranch country in the distance ahead, she stops the truck and sits for a minute, watching the hundred head of cows and their calves ambling down the road ahead of the riders, the clump thinning as the cows see unmowed grass in the ditches and lumber down to snatch a mouthful or two before the horsemen move them on. There are five riders: Nick, who is Louisa's husband of twenty-five years, their neighbour Brody Reiker, his son Cody and daughter Raeanne, and Cody's friend, Jesse. The boys, in their late teens, are wearing chaps, although it's a warm day, and here on the bald prairie there's no brush or trees they have to ride through that might scratch their legs, and spurs, although their horses are well broken and this has to be the tamest job possible—they're only moving cows and calves from a community pasture home for the winter—and Stetsons and colourful neckscarves just like in the movies. The vanity of the men has lately begun to amuse her, as if who they are as human beings is all invested in their hats.

She sighs, a little ashamed of her thoughts; she used to be as starry-eyed as the next girl when she saw one of them in all his cowboy gear. Vanity it may be, she tells herself, but at least it's harmless. After all, she grew up here, she knows as well as anybody what it really takes to stay in this life: it takes everything. It takes stuff you don't even have, she thinks. You have to be smarter than bankers and machinery dealers, and when you need to be, tougher and meaner than the lowest snake. You have to—She tells herself, *Shut up, just shut up*, jerks open the truck door, and steps out. It's Pat, she knows it. She's reminded again, fleetingly, of the young woman, Stephanie is her name, she saw Friday night at supper at the McIntosh ranch, her new baby bundled and sleeping on her lap, as if the child were a purse or a package from the store.

She stands on the dirt road for a minute and kicks at small stones, her eyes on the ground, then stretches to ease the ache out of her legs and back from hours spent sitting in the truck. On her left is the old Garrett place where Pat was raised. There isn't a soul around, it's been deserted for years, harvest is over, and the new renter lives a few miles away, over the west hills.

She wanders across the road and onto the dusty approach into the yard, past the double row of scraggly, leafless caraganas and into the farmyard proper. On her left, rising up out of the uncut crested wheat grass, is a crooked row of rusted, bent, and obsolete farm machinery that stretches back into pioneer days: a binder, an old threshing machine, even a walking plough. Standing with her hands in her jacket pockets and staring up at the house's boarded-over windows and unpainted shabbiness, she can't believe how many people once lived in it—seven kids in Pat's family. It's barely twenty feet by twenty, bigger if you count the porches. How we used to live, she thinks, and twists her neck to relieve the tension that's giving her a headache.

She steps back to the trees, and walking in between the double row of gnarled caraganas, she unzips her jeans and pulls them down and squats in the tall grass, the stiff heads of the crested wheat grass scratching her rear. Relieved, she rises, zips her jeans, and walks back onto the road.

The cattle and riders are maybe a half-mile ahead of her now. She opens the truck door, sits sideways on the driver's seat, and stares out across the road to the house. Pat was one of the older girls. Their father, drunk at the time, died in a runaway when Pat was about fifteen, and after that her mother had lost the farm. Everybody knew what a mean old bastard Jug Garrett had been. They used to pity Dorothy, Pat's mother, but nobody had ever done a thing to straighten Jug out. Pat wouldn't talk about him, never had.

"He wasn't as bad as old man Wickers," Nick had pointed out to Louisa, as if that made Jug's meanness all right. "He was so bad his boys tried to hang him. Would have too, if a neighbour hadn't come along just when they'd thrown the rope over a barn rafter."

She thinks of Pat stopping in for coffee, saying she'd fallen down the cellar stairs when Louisa exclaimed over a bruised cheek and a cut lip. And I never even suspected, she thinks, disgusted with herself. It never entered my head. She thinks how Stephanie flinched every time her young husband spoke, or even raised a hand to scratch his ear.

She looks up from her reverie to see that the cattle and riders behind them are almost at the corner where they'll stop. She gets into the truck, starts it, and drives at a good clip until she's nearly reached them. Nick and Brody have already started slowly to push the cattle to one side of the road for her. When she's opposite Raeanne, she calls out, "How's it going?"

"Okay," Raeanne tells her, not smiling—she'd rather be out somewhere with her friends, but her father has insisted she help the neighbours. No matter, Louisa is already gone, inching past the cattle, ready to brake should a calf dart out.

Raeanne is blonde, with a fifteen-year-old's cute, perfect figure. Her skin is pink and satin-smooth, so that beside her, Louisa feels like a piece of old shoe leather. Nick is smitten, Louisa sees. He's frequently smitten by very young, pretty women. Harmless, she knows, but still, it makes her angry as much because of the false idea it will give Raeanne about her power in the world as Nick never wastes any charm on her any more.

She pulls up on the grass judging which way the wind is blowing, thankfully lightly today, and positions the truck so that it acts as a buffer, parks, gets out, hauls out the big cooler, and begins to set out the food, paper plates, and plastic cutlery on the truck's end-gate. She knows without looking that the riders have moved onto the grass where she is, leaving the cattle to stand or graze. They're too tired to spread out much; these first few miles are pretty much all uphill and it's a warm day for them, nearly fifty degrees Fahrenheit.

The riders have dismounted and are loosening their cinches. Brody takes his saddle off and tosses it onto the grass, and the boys, starving as teenage boys always are, are striding toward the food, their spurs clinking. Nick is looking after Raeanne's horse, and she watches Raeanne walk toward her, her gait a bit stiff-legged, which is nothing to what it'll be by tonight, Louisa thinks.

"Hungry?" Louisa asks. She opens a thermos and fills mugs with coffee. When they're all comfortably seated on the hay bales Nick has thrown out of the truck box, munching away on their roast beef sandwiches and sipping coffee into which Nick has poured a dollop of rye from the bottle he keeps under the truck seat, Louisa asks if anybody has seen Walt Woodhouse lately.

"Why?" Nick asks, a warning to her to shut up.

"Didn't think he'd show his face," Louisa says, straight to Nick's. The two boys huddle close to each other and talk in undertones, their murmuring broken by a snicker.

Raeanne says hesitantly, "I saw him at the Credit Union on Tuesday."

Louisa tells her, "He's the one drove Pat crazy. They had to dope her and haul her away to Regina just last week." Raeanne flushes and looks at the ground, mowing the stiff grass with one boot.

"Now, now," Nick mutters, not looking at Louisa. To Brody he says, "Where'd you get that gelding? He's a nice-looking horse."

"He's off that Walker place," Brody answers. The two men continue talking and Louisa busies herself at the end-gate, covering the sandwiches with a cloth, opening another thermos of coffee. She isn't sure why she needed to tell Raeanne that—she probably knew it anyway—and it occurs to her that maybe she was using Raeanne as an excuse to let Nick know again how angry she is. Or something. She moves away from the men and then further, to the far side of the truck where she leans against the box with her back to them. After a moment she sees Raeanne has followed her. Raeanne's eyes are on Louisa's face, there's both a hesitancy and a determination in them.

"How did he … drive her crazy?" Raeanne asks. Louisa, about to be harsh, studying the girl, sees something fragile there that softens her tone.

"He hit her," she says. "Broke her ribs, she had black eyes, that sort of thing." Raeanne leans against the truck beside Louisa and the two of them gaze out over the hills to the west. Behind them, they hear the steady murmur of the men's voices.

"I guess I heard Mom say that," Raeanne says. She swings her head quickly to Louisa again. "That can drive you crazy?" she asks. "I mean …"

Louisa says, "He was mean to her in lots of other ways too." She hesitates, Raeanne is somebody else's daughter, after all, and she isn't sure if she should go on. "After years of that, last week he up and told her he had a younger woman—nobody knows if he really does or not—and Pat just—that was the last straw, I guess—she just started to babble." She looks off into the distant sky where a flock of geese are honking their disorderly way south.

Raeanne says, "I'd *never* let anybody treat me like that. If my dad ever hit my mom, she'd kill him. I mean, she'd get the twenty-two and let him have it." She laughs an embarrassed laugh, glancing sideways at Louisa as if she thinks maybe she shouldn't have said this.

Louisa says, "You stick to that, girl, you'll be okay."

"But still," Raeanne says suddenly, studying the dusty toes of her riding boots, "wasn't she crazy to stay so long? I mean, crazy in the first place? Or … whatever."

Louisa shrugs. "She seemed okay to me, except that she wouldn't leave Walt. It was like she didn't think anybody could hide her good enough from him. She didn't believe the

Mounties could keep her safe. She got so scared of him, she plumb raised him up into some giant-size demon, when he's just this dried-up, drunk, useless SOB."

"Mom says Albert Miller went to jail for beating up Ida Nixon," Raeanne tells her, but it sounds as if she's asking a question. Louisa feels a bit sorry for her, she wonders if Evelyn, her mother, ever tells her a thing.

"He's crazy," Louisa explains. "Even the Mounties could see that. He was going to kill somebody." She hesitates. "We all knew," she tells the girl, hearing the strained sound in her own voice. "Everybody knew how Walt hurt Pat, but—I don't know—it just seems like it's a hard thing to do anything about. Pat doesn't have no brothers around here any more and her father's dead—not that he would have helped her." Raeanne nods slowly, her eyes shifting away into the distant grassy slopes, where a half-dozen antelope have halted and watch them, heads up, tensed to run. "And he never did it when there was anybody around," Louisa adds. "Pat told me he used to take all the keys out of the vehicles so she couldn't get away."

Louisa suddenly remembers how Stephanie's husband hovered nearby the whole time Louisa tried to have a conversation with his wife. It's a shock to realize that he wasn't curious about her, as she'd thought, or being polite; he was making sure Stephanie didn't tell Louisa anything, that she didn't ask for help.

She pushes herself away from the truck, walks a few steps away from Raeanne, pretending to be studying the cattle. On the other side of the truck, Nick is doing the same. The cattle are moving around slowly now, instead of standing motionless or lying down. He turns back and calls to all of them, "Time to move."

Brody and the two boys slowly rise, toss out leftover coffee from their mugs, gulp down the last bite of chocolate cake, find their gloves, resettle their hats, and head toward their horses. Nick says, over the truck box, "You gonna ride, Raeanne? Or you gonna stay with Lou?" He smiles at her, his most charming, boyish smile that Louisa hasn't seen for quite a while, and she thinks, A pretty girl comes along and men lose the few brains God gave them. Raeanne hesitates, looks from Nick to Louisa and back again.

"You go have fun," Louisa tells her. She bends down, tears off a handful of grass, and wipes vigorously at a nonexistent smear of manure on her boot. She hears the swish of their boots in the grass as they walk away, but she hardly notices. Bending down, a picture has popped in front of her eyes, as clear as if she's looking at a movie: Stephanie, her face bloodied and bruised almost to unrecognizability, her stare so blank that Louisa knows she is dead. She straightens so fast that for a second she's dizzy.

Louisa and Nick are in town on business. While Nick stops in at the vet's for some advice about a sick cow, she goes to the Co-op to buy groceries. Coming out of an aisle, she almost runs her cart into a stranger's, then realizes that it's Marina McIntosh, Stephanie's mother.

"Hi, there, Lou," Marina says. For a second, Louisa can't think of a thing to say, she's seeing Marina chattering away with the other women in the kitchen that night, as if the strained face of her own daughter was just because the girl was tired from giving birth. She occupies herself jockeying her cart out of the way, her lips already stretched into a smile she doesn't mean, before she can look at Marina and say hello. There's a pause and Louisa asks, "How is … Stephanie?" as if she'd momentarily forgotten her name.

Marina says, "Good, she's really good. Baby's growing like a weed." Louisa studies her face, looking for some sign, but sees nothing.

"They grow fast," she says and hesitates, wanting to say something, anything, to Marina about the danger she believes Stephanie to be in. But in the end she just can't muster the courage, and after a second, Marina pushes her cart on down the next aisle. By the time Louisa has found everything on her list, Marina has finished checking out her groceries, loaded them into her truck, and driven away.

Louisa leaves her bags of groceries at the store to be picked up on her way out of town and goes to the café to meet Nick. She finds him sitting on a stool at the coffee bar among a row of his friends. He sees her come in and after a while he moves to the booth she's taken.

"Get everything you wanted?" he asks. She nods, not speaking or looking at him. "Something the matter?"

"No." She glances up at him. Under the wide brim of his Stetson his face has gone stiff, he's expecting a complaint from her eventually. She smiles tentatively, reminding herself that, after all, none of this is Nick's fault.

The outer door opens and Walt Woodhouse comes in. He sits down on the stool Nick has just vacated and says a loud "Hello." Soon the conversation among the men starts up again. Louisa knows her face is reddening; she's so angry the large plastic menu is quivering in her hands. Nick says nothing, but he clears his throat nervously, or else he's warning her to calm down.

Louisa wants to leave, she wants to stare hard at Walt and then go out, banging the door behind her. She wonders what would happen if every woman in the café—there are four of them—pointedly got up and walked out when Walt came in, if they kept doing that, if it would do any good. Abruptly, she tosses down the menu, gets up, walks fast down the aisle between the rows of booths, her boots making a racket, and goes into the bathroom, slamming the door. Behind her, she knows, Nick will be studying the menu very hard.

On the way home Nick says, "So what the hell's bothering you."

"You know," she says, after a minute. He moves his hands on the steering wheel, as if he doesn't know where to place them.

"You know I'm really sorry about that," he says, meaning what has happened to Pat. Louisa wants to say, *If you and the other men would have stopped Walt—if you wouldn't have anything to do with him now*—but she forbids herself. The men have their own code, not that she likes it, but she can't expect Nick to change it all by himself. She says softly, "Nick?"

"What?" he asks, glancing at her, not sure whether he should smile.

"Stephanie McIntosh—I mean Stephanie Degler now ..." Nick waits. "I saw Marina at the Co-op. She doesn't seem to even know—"

"Know what?" Nick asks, a touch of impatience entering his voice. Louisa throws caution to the winds.

"That she's being abused by that Rory she married." Nick doesn't say anything for a minute, but his touch on the wheel seems to grow lighter, more careful.

"How do you know? Did she tell you? Stephanie, I mean." Louisa shakes her head no. She tells him what she saw that night while he and the other men were chewing the fat on the soft chairs in the living room and the women sat together in the kitchen.

"He kept coming and going, you know?" Louisa says. "And I think he was keeping an eye on her to make sure she wouldn't tell us about him." Nick takes a hand off the steering wheel and mops his face with it, a gesture he only makes when he's tired or worried. He sets it back on the steering wheel.

"I don't know what to do," Louisa says.

"It's none of our business," he says, surprised.

"I could go to that new Mountie in town," she says, as much to see what he'll say as because she thinks she'll be able to do this.

"What could he do?" Nick asks. "He couldn't do nothing without some evidence or a complaint from her or her folks—"

"Warn him!" she says to Nick, her voice vibrating with emotion. "He could go check it out, maybe put some fear into that Rory, maybe slow him down some—"

"Hey," Nick says, his voice softening. "Take it easy, Lou."

"Nick," she says, she's begging now, "I can't get her out of my mind, I can't sleep for thinking about her—"

"No," Nick says, his voice firm, "It's up to her family, not us."

Louisa has spent the day in the city visiting Pat in the halfway house she's been moved to from the psychiatric ward. It's nearly midnight by the time she gets home, and although Nick's truck is parked by the door, the house is dark. When she enters the bedroom, he clicks on his bedside lamp.

"How was she?"

"Terrible," Louisa says. "Drugged to the gills. Could hardly talk." She sits down in the chair at the foot of the bed and kicks off one shoe. "I invited her to come and stay with us when she's well enough."

"That'll bring Walt down on our heads," Nick says. Louisa throws her other shoe against the closet door, leaving a dent in the wood.

"You men let him get away with it. You treated him like he was just one of the boys too. Like it didn't matter to you one bit." They are partway into a very bad row; Nick has sat up on the side of the bed, ready to start shouting back. They glare at each other through the lamplight's glow.

Seeing suddenly how he has aged in the wrinkles in his neck and the lines around his mouth, remembering him telling his own daughters they had to get an education, get away from here, Louisa's anger slowly deserts her. She says quietly to him, "She'll never be okay, Nick. She's just—wrecked."

He puts out his hand to her, she moves to sit beside him and he places his arm around her waist, pulling her against him, turning his face into her hair.

"I'm sorry," he says. "You know how sorry I am. I always liked Pat, I *wanted* to …" He tightens his grasp and for a long moment she leans into him, her face pressed against his work-hardened chest.

Nick gets back into bed and Louisa finishes undressing. She pulls on her nightgown and slides in beside him. In a moment, he's snoring. Louisa lies with her eyes open in the dark, but instead of seeing Pat, she sees Stephanie, how she never smiled, never moved from her chair, how—it seems now to Louisa—she gave off a mute suffering, that surely she couldn't have been the only one in the kitchen who felt it.

She thinks, In the morning I'll go to the Mountie. But if the Mountie goes there and everybody finds out, as they always do, that I sent him, Rory will come gunning for me; Marina and Harry will never speak to me or Nick again for shaming them; then Nick will be furious. She moves her legs roughly under the covers and Nick turns over, mumbling.

But Stephanie's face won't leave her, her mind won't stop going around and around. Finally, she decides: she'll drive down to the Degler place herself and pay Stephanie a visit, just a visit—to see the baby, she'll say. She'll do it when Nick is off at the last calf sale of the season over in Victory. He doesn't need to know. And if she gets the chance, she'll make it clear to

Stephanie that she, Louisa, knows what's going on. If she gets the chance, that's what she'll do.

As Louisa drives south down the grid toward the Deglers' isolated farm, it's cloudy and threatening to snow, and in the distance it's hard to tell where land leaves off and sky begins. She's not afraid, but nervous, her palms are damp inside her mitts and her shoulder and neck muscles tense. She keeps reminding herself that almost certainly Rory will have gone to the calf sale with all the other men, that she doesn't have to do anything more than pay a friendly visit. But the tension doesn't go away.

The Degler place looks deserted, there isn't a vehicle anywhere in sight, although there are a few tracks in the snow. The old frame house, once yellow, needs paint, the bottom step on the porch is broken, and seeing all this, for a second Louisa is tempted to turn around and go back home. I've come all this way, she tells herself, I can't quit now.

She gets out of her truck slowly and mounts the steps, and the blue heeler chained by the door snarls and barks. She goes into the porch, its floor has shifted so that the outer door doesn't close any more, and knocks loudly. After a long pause, the door slowly opens a few inches and Stephanie's face appears in the crack.

"Hi, there, Stephanie," Louisa says. Inexplicably, at the sight of the girl she feels the tension that's been growing in her leave, and she goes on casually, "I was just on my way down to Smith's, thought I'd stop in and see that baby of yours." Stephanie has the door open only about a foot, she appears frightened, but at the mention of the baby, she says hesitantly, "Hello, Louisa." She doesn't sound surprised to see her, she doesn't sound anything at all. But she opens the door wide enough for Louisa to enter the kitchen and steps back. She seems diminished, surely she's lost weight since the night Louisa saw her at Stephanie's parents' ranch? There is not a touch of colour in her face. Even her lips are pale.

Louisa asks cheerily, "Rory not home?"

"He's gone to Victory—to the calf sale," Stephanie says. She's holding both her hands in front of her, twisting them together nervously. She looks around her spotless, shabby kitchen, as if she can't remember just what it is she should do now. "Would you … like some coffee?" I bet she's not supposed to have visitors, Louisa thinks.

"Oh, okay," she says. "I have to get on over to Lisa's, but I guess I got time for coffee." She wants to calm Stephanie, so that she'll drop her guard, maybe talk to her. Louisa doesn't know what will happen then, but she came to try to help, and she'll stick it out until she finds a way. She sits down at the wobbly kitchen table, remarks on the weather, says she hopes prices at the sale are good, while Stephanie puts the coffee on. When it's dripping through its filter, she asks to see the baby. Stephanie almost smiles. She goes out of the room—how quiet she is, she doesn't make a sound—and comes back quickly with her baby, Tara is her name, in her arms.

Louisa takes the baby and coos to her, tells Stephanie how pretty she is, how she's growing like a weed, although the little face looks pale to her. But while Stephanie pours the coffee into mugs, sets them on the table, Louisa feels her composure slipping away from her. It's the baby's weightlessness, the way she's too still, too quiet, like her mother. Sweat is breaking out on her forehead; she has to duck her head so Stephanie doesn't notice how fast she's begun to breathe.

"I have to feed her," Stephanie says, in that same quiet, emotionless voice, and stands. Louisa hands her the baby, she's gotten a grip on herself again, and Stephanie goes back to her place, sits, and begins to unbutton her neat cotton blouse so the baby can nurse.

Louisa says carefully, "Everything okay here?" Stephanie's fingers on the blouse buttons give a little jerk.

She says quickly, "Sure, fine, everything's fine."

"Don't try to kid me, Steph," Louisa says. "I can see how things are." Stephanie freezes, looks at Louisa with a terror-stricken expression. "He's gone for the day, Stephanie," she reminds her. "He can't hear this—"

"Sometimes he comes back." This bursts out of Stephanie in a high, breathless voice, while her eyes flit to the door and back to fix themselves on Louisa.

"If you want," Louisa says, keeping her voice as calm as she can manage, "you can come with me right now. Just bundle up that baby and we'll go. He'll never know where you went."

Now colour floods Stephanie's pale cheeks, she's breathing quickly, and she puts the baby up against her shoulder, hugging her, as if the child will be a shield between her and Louisa.

"I can't just—I can't—"

"Of course you can," Louisa says. She's found the right tone now, self-assured, collected, so firm as to brook no disagreement. "You don't have to live like this. He's got no right—"

"He's my husband," Stephanie whispers. She still hasn't taken her eyes away from Louisa's face. Louisa wants to say what she thinks of Rory, but holds it back, and just shakes her head slowly, no, as if Stephanie is, quite simply, wrong.

"Get your coat and a warm blanket for Tara and we'll go. Go on, now." Stephanie still stares at her, clutching her baby, but Louisa sees in the way Stephanie's composure is going that she can win this. "Hurry, now," she adds in a friendly way, almost conversationally. "Be quick about it."

The girl stands clumsily, noisily, lowering her baby to the

crook of her arm—it's then that Louisa sees the dark bruises on her neck—and whispers, "You better go, Louisa."

Louisa stands, too, careful to move slowly. "Give me Tara. You run and get some diapers." She reaches for the baby. "You hurry, now," she says again.

There's a long moment when they stare at each other mutely, Stephanie's eyes large and glittering with something that might be the awakening of hope, Louisa trying to keep her gaze steady and confident. Then, her eyes still locked to Louisa's, Stephanie hands her the baby.

As they go out of the house and get in the truck it's snowing; judging by the thin drifts of snow on the hood and windshield, it must have started when Louisa went into the Degler house. She backs around and drives away, out of the yard, and at the grid, points the truck north. It occurs to Louisa that they're leaving tracks. Never mind, by the time Rory gets back from the sale, they'll be covered up or they'll have blown away.

They're not two miles north of the Deglers' farm when they meet a pickup driving south fast, but the snowfall is thicker now, and with it billowing up as the vehicles meet and pass, Louisa can't tell who the driver is. Stephanie has her face buried in her baby's blanket, Louisa doesn't know if crying or praying, or what. She steps on the gas, but visibility is too poor, so she drops her speed back to an even eighty klicks.

"I heard there's a safe house over in Victory. Bars, locks, the Mounties guard it." Louisa doesn't know if the part about the Mounties is true, but she doesn't care. "You'll be safe there," she adds. Stephanie puts a free hand up to her face, then puts it down again. She hasn't spoken since she got into the truck.

Suddenly, it seems out of nowhere, Louisa sees a half-ton has pulled out of the curtain of falling snow and is riding their bumper. She's about to slow and pull over so it can pass, when the driver pulls out, roars past them, then, braking, slides his truck in front of them at an angle, cutting them off. Louisa brakes hard. Her truck fishtails on the frozen gravel, bouncing over the ruts, and jerks to a halt a foot from the half-ton's side.

Beside her, Stephanie has begun to gulp air, letting out short screams with each breath, like a woman in labour. She's clutching the baby so tight that the child starts to shriek too. The driver's door of the half-ton opens and Rory Degler gets out, facing them, his left hand setting something along the top of the seat so they can see it through the back window. It's a rifle. He passes Louisa, squeezes between her hood and his truck's side, still facing them, goes to Stephanie's side, and opens her door.

Stephanie has stopped screaming, but she's shaking so hard that as she tries to step down to the road he has to grab her jacket to keep her from falling. He isn't even looking at her; he's looking at Louisa with his wide, light blue eyes. She stares back, fascinated; she can't look away; she can't tell what she feels, although she doesn't think it's fear—it's something else; it's as if in his gaze she's encountering something fascinating, something she's never met before.

Behind him, Stephanie has opened the door of her husband's truck, slides the screaming baby in on the seat, stumbling twice, tries to get in, succeeds finally, and pulls the door shut. Louisa sees this out of the corner of her eye, because she can't take her eyes from Rory's. He stares into Louisa's for another long minute: there is some moving darkness in his pale eyes, some blackness that she can see, and whatever it is it pulls at her insides, it both scares her and—

Abruptly, without closing her passenger door, he turns and walks away. He gets back into the driver's seat, slams the door, guns the motor, does a series of rapid partial turns on the narrow road until his truck is facing back south, steps on the gas, his tires spewing gravel that hits Louisa's truck with a series of angry thuds that make her flinch, and vanishes behind her into the wall of falling snow.

Louisa sits in the truck, her hands flat on her thighs, staring through the windshield as the snow piles up on the wipers. She finds herself shaking, but she ignores this. Her mind is racing: she'll go to the Mountie, swear Degler threatened to shoot her—but Stephanie will lie for him, what else can she do? *Now,* she'll go to Stephanie's parents—A huge anger is rising in her, her chest swells with rage, and for a long moment she can't breathe.

I will kill him myself, she thinks. Shocked, she lifts her hands abruptly from her thighs, holding them in mid-air for an instant, and then sets them on the icy steering wheel.

The passenger door is still open and a thin drift of snow is settling on the seat. She slides over, brushes the snow out, and pulls the door shut, then moves back into the driver's seat and sits there, not moving. Her rage, her astonishment, her determination—even her pity—have left her, and she is no longer trembling. It is as if for the first time in her life she's felt the force of gravity. It has entered her through her pores, it sits like a steady rock inside her, lending her a new weightiness, a new, grave sobriety.

Her mind sweeps across the peaceful, snow-covered prairie to the deserted-looking farm and ranch houses, to the cattle and horses standing in corrals, snow building up on their backs and manes, to the homely village miles down the road full of people she's known all her life, going about their business, as if—as if they've never seen, never even guessed at the existence of what she just saw in Rory Degler's eyes.

Postmodernism

Today Lawrence leaves for Africa. I know he is leaving and where he is going because he told me when we had drinks together the other night in the mall near his parents' apartment in a senior citizens' high-rise. He had not seen his parents in a very long time and I think he does not expect to see them again in this life. He has come to say goodbye. It is too bad because they are very old and he is their only child.

Lawrence and I have been divorced for fifteen years, but even though I've been married to someone else for most of that time, and have children with him, I still love Lawrence.

I don't think he loves me. It is worse than that: he loves no one. "I no longer have relationships with women," he tells me. In that particular wording I do not read homosexuality; he is telling me he has become celibate.

I am a writer and I have been accused of merely writing autobiography in my stories, as if that were somehow easier to do than making everything up. Before I went to meet Lawrence, agitated as I was, it crossed my mind that I would find some way of writing about seeing him after so many years—the things we say to each other, what has become of us—some peripheral telling of lies maybe, or an extension of fact that will take the encounter from the banal to the cosmic, that will find a universal chord, because that is what good writers do, the ones who know there is no difference among autobiography, biography, fiction or non-fiction, between stories and real life.

Even after so many years, when we met we didn't touch, although we moved close to each other as if we thought we should or wanted to. Or maybe it was only the normal social urge to shake hands or hug or brush cheeks. But we didn't, both speaking at once about going inside the bar or going somewhere else or being sorry to be late or I'm always early.

Lawrence has been in an ashram in New Mexico, near Los Alamos, for the last fifteen years, and I was surprised at how much he drank, no polite nursing a light beer, but three, maybe four whiskies and more, that he smoked the entire time we were together. "I didn't think they allowed that in an ashram," I said to him, trying to be wry, amused by his life choices, sort of removed from him, as if he was someone I barely knew, instead of the person whose physical presence in my life is inconsequential because, although I tried for ten years to erase him from my memory, he had become, when I wasn't looking, a part of my very essence, of the inescapable texture of my soul. Such is his presence in my life that though Lawrence and I have no children, I am not surprised to find that my two with my second husband look a little like Lawrence. At least I see Lawrence in them every day. For obvious reasons I've never told anybody this.

"They don't," he said, and looked at his cigarette in something of the way I must have been looking at him, as if it were an independent creature that had lit itself and sprung into his fingers, he couldn't quite think how, but accepted the fact with resignation, just another manifestation of Buddha. "I don't smoke or drink when I'm there." We were silent, remembering the long-ago nights drinking in the bar with friends, the pub we said then, when we were students. I've sometimes thought

Lawrence had a drinking problem, he certainly drank a lot when we were young, before drugs came along. I drink more now, though, than I ever did then, and as for drugs, I hated them. By the time they were part of our lives I was getting tired. I wanted only to go home and sleep, or to go for a solitary walk down a country lane.

I had set myself, before our meeting, to be removed from him, cool, I had shut off my heart—don't laugh—anyone who has suffered, really suffered, can do this. I don't know if it's a good thing or not. But I knew I had to protect myself from him because I knew I still loved him, that I will go to my grave loving him more, not less, every year. It is no fault of mine.

Now Lawrence is a holy man and I, a writer, am learning the niceties of moderate fame, the dimensions and intricacies of it, the protocol, you might say. I want to ask him about holiness, how it feels, the spiritual life; I want him to take out his heart, open it, and lay it out on the table so I can see the wheels and cogs, the turning of it. I imagine the parts as dull brass, worn, but with glints of gold moving against a rosy background. I can see us sitting there, bent over it as it lies open on the brown bar table. We stare at it in silence, Lawrence adjusting the glasses he now wears, me perhaps surreptitiously taking out the small pad and stubby pencil I always carry, scribbling a note in the shorthand I have invented that nobody else can read.

But I thought it was better to go for particulars.

"Why don't you have relationships with women?" I asked him.

It was gloomy in the bar, the way that bars are deliberately badly lit so that customers will let down their guards, feel an intimacy with each other, with the waitress and the bartender, feel for a while safe, so that they won't want to leave. It was a small place and there were only a few people scattered in twos and threes at the other tables. I moved closer to Lawrence so we could talk without being overheard. In this small city, my hometown, strangers know me.

"Because I'm too destructive with them," Lawrence replied, as if it cost him little to say this, only a hesitation giving him away. I wanted to ask him, Do you still love me? but I didn't. I knew he would say he does, and I knew, too, that this would be true, but in such a way as to be of no use to me. That is one thing I have learned in the fifteen years without him.

Lawrence rarely looked at me, while I leaned close to him and didn't take my eyes off him. He told me he was being sent by his "community" to Somalia to work with the hungry. It occurred to me that Los Alamos would be the perfect place for the Second Coming of Christ. I said this.

"An apparition out of the desert in silver boots," I suggested.

"With bright blue eyes," Lawrence added. "Not milky brown ones."

"A white chiffon scarf around his neck, blowing in the wind from the atomic blast," I offered.

"You're thinking of Wayne Newton," he said.

"No, Sam Shepard in *The Right Stuff.*"

I didn't like what was happening. I hated talking to him as if he were just an old friend, I hated the way he wouldn't say the things I'd waited fifteen years to hear, but I knew I would hate it more if he said them. I began to think the meeting was a mistake for both of us, although how could it be?

Thinking about it afterwards, or rather, trying to write about it, I want the Lawrence character to say to the woman, "Are you happy?" He didn't though, and I realize now that the question comes from movies or second-rate novels. It is perhaps the one question real people would never ask each other. It is too intimate, too hard to answer, too much to ask of anyone. In fact, it occurs to me it is a silly question, as if happiness were a steady state one might finally rest in through judicious life choices.

Looking at Lawrence, I can see that fifteen years in an ashram, learning to be holy, making holy choices, have not made him happy. As for me, marrying again and having children and a career, although I am not unhappy, have made me lose track of what happiness is. Of what I once thought it was, when I was young and thought I knew with clarity what it is and, of course, that it was achievable. It seems so strange to me now that I didn't notice then that no one older than me was happy, that no matter how others behaved, when they looked away their eyes grew dark.

When Lawrence phoned and asked me to come out and have a drink with him, I didn't ask him why. Another silly question that a screenwriter or playwright, imagining this occasion, might put into the mouth of a character. But not asking him why, believing I knew why, didn't mean that I knew what to expect. My heart had behaved erratically from the moment I'd heard his voice. I fluctuated from seconds of a rage so deep I had frightened myself to an aching desire that was worse. Having settled on distancing myself, when I saw the sadness in the set of his face, I was glad that I didn't care that he isn't happy.

When I stood waiting for him outside the bar and saw him come around the corner, my first thought was of how he was smaller than I remembered in every visible way, thinner and shorter, altogether diminished physically. I didn't mind that he was smaller, it was only that I half expected it in the way the farmhouse kitchen was smaller than I remembered and the convent full of killer nuns where I had the misfortune to begin school. But when I said to him that he was thin and asked, "Are you well?"—now that is a reasonable question, authors—he said that he runs five miles a day and works out, that he has never been so fit. And there was a flicker of something in his eyes beyond pride; I suspect it was delight.

I leaned closer, trying to see him clearly in the bad light and shadows.

"Do you remember the time we went to Banff and Lake Louise for that weekend without telling anybody?" he asked.

"In a borrowed car," I said, looking wryly off toward the glass wall where, in a better light, people were walking by. "And you broke your arm—"

"And it blizzarded for three days and we couldn't leave—"

"And Gerry never forgave us for not getting his car back for a week—"

But what I remembered was that thirty years ago there was no place more beautiful than Lake Louise buried in snow, the lodge half closed, nobody around. I remember especially that the only sound had been water trickling at the edge of the lake where for some reason it hadn't frozen over. And Banff not yet a tacky, tourist-ridden, expensive fake, but a real town where people went quietly about their lives. But it clings to me, over all these years, the distant crystalline sound of running water in the frozen, snowy wilderness.

"The last time I was at Lake Louise you couldn't see that famous view for people. This is not hyperbole," I said, but I could see he wasn't listening. I found I didn't want to talk about Banff. All right, I said, to all the bad authors of the world. All right.

"Why did you want to meet me?" I knew I sounded irritable. I was surprised at the quickness of his reply, as if he'd asked himself that question and had memorized the answer.

"I missed you," he said. "You were an important part of my life and I missed you." I found I didn't know what that meant. Was it an oblique way of saying he loves me? Or was it a way of saying he doesn't love me, never did? Or was he thinking he had to tie up all the loose ends because he would never be back again, that he would stay the rest of his life in Africa, that soldiers would shoot him, or he would contract a disease, that he would die there?

I realized with the detached part of myself that the group of social workers who had just seated themselves at the next table recognized me. They murmured to themselves and I heard my name. I wasn't sure how I felt about that, or how I knew they were social workers. I filed that away to mull over another time.

I didn't want to reply to Lawrence's remark. It was too terrible. I remembered suddenly him turning from me, crying in that awful way men used to cry, as if crying were like giving birth, saying, "It seems to me that everything I've ever wanted …" And what did I feel, because I had refused him something and caused him finally to cry? I think I felt somewhat pleased with myself, and astonished, not being acquainted yet with a world where you expected to get what you want.

But then he'd been angry, scathing over my dogged virginity. It was no use though, I was still too attached to my parents, my mother in particular, to recognize any man's claims on me, even one I genuinely loved. Looking back, I felt only shame, shame and wonder at the stupidity of that young girl I once was. It made me wonder if I ever knew what love was, or what it was for.

Lawrence was still not looking at me and I wondered if he remembered how much we'd once loved each other, after we'd gotten over that hurdle, and whatever others there were that I'd forgotten. Is escaping the past his reason for going to Africa? But that would be out of a romance novel and I could see he hadn't a romantic notion left in him, any more than I have. We are long past that sort of thing, the two of us.

"Why did you come?" Lawrence asked, and I thought, Now that is a question I wouldn't have thought of if I'd been writing this scene. I almost told him that, but one of my failings is my desire to be charmingly shocking, and something powerful was taking over between us. It was in the air, making it thick and hard to breathe, the darkness was deepening, and in the shadows his face grew more beautiful; perhaps what I thought was sadness was instead a kind of wisdom. I resisted my shallowness, knowing I am capable of more. It took me a minute to frame my answer.

"Because I still love you," and rage boiled up in me again and I wanted to hit him. But pity for him hushed me. At least I didn't have to go to Africa.

I wanted to pay attention then, to how I felt: I held still and concentrated on what was going on inside me. For too many years I was in too big a hurry, I sped through my feelings, I hadn't time to absorb one when I was off in another one. No wonder I never knew what I thought; I didn't even know what I felt. And the world, when I was young, was such a mystery to me. I never anticipated anything; it seemed to me that life had no form or pattern that I could discern, no clear spots, only darkness and shadow and unexpectedness. I stumbled from place to place doing pratfalls like a clown, tripping over things that weren't there, bumping into invisible walls I might have walked through, hiding in terror from the trivial and courting wide-eyed the dangerous.

I am no longer afraid, and if I still don't understand, at least experience has made me better at prediction.

And surprisingly, he didn't say anything. He only blinked and, I thought, resisted the urge to look away. I saw I had wounded him. Why should I care about his suffering? I asked myself.

It was on the day he phoned me and asked me to meet him for a drink that I realized that it is an invariable law of the universe that whatever one wants the most is always the one thing that one cannot, not ever, have. That this is the nature of desire, it seems to me a good thing to finally realize. Looking at

Lawrence, I thought this must be something he knows too, that this must be the reason he is going to Africa.

But then, before I felt fully arrived, we were parting. Lawrence butted out his cigarette, and I saw by the gesture, a certain finality to the movement of his wrist, that he had just again renounced smoking. He leaned back, coughed, gave me a funny, wavering smile. Did I smile back?

We rose, walked single file out the door, Lawrence first, then me, because my purse strap had caught on the table's corner and I stopped to free it. We stepped outside into the deserted hall and faced each other. Lawrence moved toward me as if to hug me, but a mean part of me resisted. The thought that I would probably never see him again freed me from my own unyielding nature and I allowed him to hug me, even hugged him back a little.

"Well," he said, "I'll write." I didn't say anything, though I wished he wouldn't, but then I thought, He probably won't anyway. We said something more, maybe it was goodbye, and he turned and walked away. I watched him cross the cavernous mall. I was thinking about postmodernism.

Although I suppose you could say that as a writer I've sometimes achieved postmodernism, and though I can explain it fairly clearly, I've never really understood its nature. I thought, Maybe this, in the end, is really all it is about, that hoping to find in others a reflection of ourselves that will at last make everything clear, we discover instead that, like trying to understand love, we find there is only a bottomless spiral into blackness.

But I noticed, even while I was standing there watching Lawrence walk away and disappear through the revolving doors, and even longer, as if they might suddenly reverse and push him back to me, that while I needed to see every second of his leaving, he did not, not even once, look back at me.

Light

The sign reads, "If you've been waiting more than forty-five minutes, report to staff." Lucia and Elaine have been waiting an hour when finally Lucia rises, walks down the hall to the desk, and points this out to the uniformed woman there. The woman replies briskly, not looking at Lucia, "We know you're waiting." Then less harshly, "It won't be long now." Lucia says, "I'm only telling you because of the sign."

"Mmmmm," the woman says, snapping shut a drawer, and Lucia realizes she has once again entered can't-win-land. As she reseats herself beside Elaine she tells herself that this is quite possibly funny, that some day she may laugh about it.

She reaches over and takes Elaine's small, slightly polio-deformed, very white hand in hers. Elaine grasps hers tightly, although otherwise she doesn't move or change her expression. She sits in her wheelchair, the clear plastic of her oxygen nose-piece glistening on her upper lip, ignoring even the television, normally her favourite source of entertainment, that blats away next to her.

Every chair in the waiting area is occupied by patients or their companions. Nobody speaks, except for the occasional hurried whisper, nobody laughs, nobody watches the television, though nobody turns it off either, nobody stretches and yawns and shifts position, or paces up and down. Nobody moves. They sit quietly, hands in lap, looking at nothing. All of them, both the men and women, look faded to Lucia, blurred at the edges, as if they've been out in the damp too long. Soon, after their trials here at the cancer clinic, Lucia thinks, they'll dissolve into the Great Beyond, which now, after too many hours spent waiting here, appears to Lucia to be, instead of the sunshine-dappled, flower-dotted meadow of her childhood belief, a kind of Buddhistic nothing.

She can always tell the new patients. They talk too much, they talk incessantly, a bright jabbering that disturbs the whole waiting room and which they themselves, gazing around helplessly, their eyes flitting from patient to patient and back again, seem powerless to stop. Whenever it has happened, Lucia has been annoyed by it, refusing to meet the prattlers' eyes in order to avoid responding. Now it occurs to her that these women— she's never seen a man act this way—are simply afraid, they're driven by terror, that they'll stop when the system has slowly transmuted it into the numb acquiescence of everybody else here. Since she began looking after Elaine, she finds such moments of illumination gratifying.

Weeks ago, on a weekend trip home, she'd told George about the babbling women. They were lying side by side in bed, the blinds closed against the stars and moon, the world shrunk down to this darkened intimacy.

"I miss you," he said.

"You can't imagine how they look," she said. "Aren't you getting lots of work done? It isn't forever, after all. I'll be home soon."

"How's that?" he asked, surprised. "Have you found a facility for her?" This silenced her. At this stage, no facility would take Elaine, she isn't sick enough or helpless enough yet, and if one would, Elaine would refuse to go. Lucia knew very well she'd never force her sister to go.

"I don't know," she said finally. She didn't want to tell George that so far it had all been pretty interesting. Or that she was avoiding looking into the future, except to pray silently for something to happen that would rescue her from this task before things got too bad, although she doesn't really know what too bad might be.

Eventually, Elaine's name is called and Lucia wheels her to a treatment room, helps the nurse transfer her to an easy chair so large it dwarfs Elaine's small, twisted body. They cover her with a red mohair throw Lucia has brought from the apartment—the clinic provides only flannel sheets for warmth—and the treatment commences.

Waiting, while Elaine lies with closed eyes in the easy chair, an alarming, if also rather pretty, red fluid flowing down tubing into a needle planted in her arm, Lucia notices a tall thin man in a hospital dressing gown walk slowly past the open door. For a second he seems merely familiar, and then she realizes he's the husband of one of George's colleagues, someone she's known for years. It's so unusual to see somebody she knows here that, without reflection, she gets up and hurries after him.

She finds him around a corner in a niche. He's seated on a hard wooden lab chair, his arm is extended on the chair's wide shelf-like projection, a nurse is pushing up the sleeve of his dressing gown, about to apply the tourniquet, when Lucia bends over him, grinning, and says softly, "We've got to stop meeting like this."

He glances at her, slowly, his irises are a pale, flat blue, the pupils shrunk to the tiniest points of darkness. His mouth is fixed in a half-smile, and he says nothing, nor does his expression change. She thinks he hasn't heard what she's said, more, that although only two weeks earlier on a weekend at home she'd had dinner at his house, he doesn't know who she is. She touches his shoulder lightly with her palm, an apology, a commiseration, then turns and hurries back to Elaine. She feels oddly elated, if puzzled, and when finally she recognizes that absent half-smile as another manifestation of the fear that lurks in every corner and shadow in this bright new facility, she's ashamed, as if to joke—although isn't that what everyone says you're supposed to do?—were immoral, or at the very least, a glaring faux pas.

More, she's astonished. Elaine was born with moderate mental retardation, then felled further by childhood polio, she can't read, she has no formal education and only the narrowest of life experience, while her friend is a well-travelled, much-honoured professor. Mulling this over as she waits for the bag of bright fluid to empty into Elaine's arm, she can't get over how here in the cancer clinic everything is instructive.

Back in Elaine's apartment, with Elaine sleeping from the anti-nausea medication, her oxygen concentrator running noisily at her bedside, Lucia does housework. The few dishes washed, the few square feet of vinyl in the walk-through kitchen swept, she decides against dusting. She ought to be resting while Elaine sleeps, the first post-chemo night can be harrowing, but the more tired she is, the harder she finds it to sleep. She tells herself that the moment will come when she's so tired she'll sleep like a baby.

The muted roar of the oxygen concentrator in the bedroom on the other side of the wall disturbs her rest too. It can't be turned off, Elaine's lips would turn blue and she'd gasp for breath, her lung cancer is well advanced now, nor can it be muffled by putting it in a closet because its electrical cord is too short and the oxygen-supply people, who come periodically to exchange the portable tanks Elaine uses whenever she leaves the apartment, are adamantly against extension cords. Wherever Elaine is in the apartment, the concentrator is never more than a few feet away. Lucia often thinks that its drone would do nicely as background to the torturing of the wicked in hell.

She should phone George. Talking with him reminds her that she won't be here in Elaine's apartment in this city five hours from her own forever, that she hasn't yet joined the ranks of the condemned. Otherwise, as the weeks pass, she finds this easier and easier to forget.

But George won't be home yet, so she puts the phone down, picks up her book from the stack she keeps behind the kitchen door—the apartment is so small that with two occupying it there's no place left to put them—stretches out on the sofa, and opens her book. George, an English professor, has just finished a stint on a non-fiction literary jury. He's been keeping her supplied with reading material from the more than two hundred new books he's had to read. But on her last trip home she'd found herself rejecting a highly praised memoir by a poet, a biography of a movie star, a humorous book about small-town life, everything that George had already selected for her.

"What's the matter with these?" he'd asked her in surprise.

"It's just that … they just don't look very interesting." They'd stared at the wall of books in front of them. Tentatively, Lucia reached out, took a thin volume from the shelf, and flipped through its pages.

"That's about the Holocaust," he told her briskly, reaching to take it from her.

"I know it," she'd said, evading his reach to put it aside on the table between them. In the end she'd collected a half-dozen books about the Holocaust from his shelves.

"They're pretty depressing reading," he warned her. "Especially now."

"I don't care," she said. "I just … want to."

But once she'd put the books in a bag and was setting it by her suitcase, he'd handed her a paper on which he'd scribbled the titles and authors of a half-dozen more.

"Those books will tell you the story," he explained, nodding down at the bookbag. "But none of them are works of art, and they have in common a failure to express the full scope of what happened." She watched him, as always, half irritated, half admiring of this professorial mode he often fell into with her. "The books on this list will help you …" he hesitated, "come to terms," he added finally, shrugging, as if such a thing were hardly possible. Then he'd looked hard into her eyes, as if she were one of his students about whose talents he was slightly dubious.

She'd begun with a memoir by a Canadian woman, a Jew born in Poland of a many-branched, tightly knit, prosperous family, nearly all of whom were killed in concentration camps. In it, the memoirist tells of her return in late adulthood to seek out the old family home, to find any remaining living relatives, to visit family graves if they can be found, and, most of all, to revisit the sites of her blissful early childhood, all of this in an attempt to sort out these happy memories from what she knows only by hearsay to be, for most of her family, their tragic outcome. It is an interesting enough narrative, although Lucia doesn't really understand the memoirist's impulse to make such a journey and then, especially, to write a book about it.

But she hasn't much left to read, and as she makes her way through to the end, and the full realization of what happened to the writer's grandparents, her aunts and uncles, her cousins, to the beautiful house in the countryside where her happiest memories reside, comes crashing over the author, Lucia thinks, What a fool the writer was to want to know.

She sets the book down on the sofa beside her and stares out the double-glass doors onto the small balcony that overlooks the parking lot, then a service station, and beyond that, one of the busiest of the city's downtown streets. She knows she's being mean-spirited, even childish. Of course the woman needed to know. She wonders about the word "needed," but in the other room, over the concentrator's loud hum, Elaine has begun to cough and Lucia drops the book and hurries in to her.

In the absence of a hospital bed, which Elaine becomes nearly hysterical at the mere mention of, Lucia has bought an item the home care people call a "wedge" because of its shape, a huge piece of foam rubber, textured so it will stay where it's placed in the bed, and on which Lucia then arranges another half-dozen pillows, so that Elaine can sleep comfortably, sitting up. If in her sleep she moves, dislodges the pillows, and begins, over the hours, slowly to sink to a flatter position in the bed, it's only a matter of minutes before she wakes, unable to breathe, coughing, gasping for breath, but too weak to sit up without help. Some nights this happens three or four times, when Lucia, hearing the first cough, on her feet before she's even awake, rushes into the bedroom, calling, "It's all right, I'm coming, it's okay," during the seconds it takes her to reach Elaine's bedside.

She puts one arm behind Elaine's back and another in the crook of her knees while Elaine pushes against the bed with her hands to assist Lucia in dragging her back up to a sitting position. All this done in semi-darkness—the city lights never allow absolute darkness in the apartment no matter what Lucia tries—and fast, before Elaine loses consciousness.

Often Lucia can't get a proper grip, can't seem to make any difference, and then she climbs onto the bed, kneels beside Elaine, and struggles until she's managed to drag her upright.

Then she goes back to the cot she sets up nightly in the living room, picks up her book, and reads until her heart stops its rapid pounding in her ears and throat and wrists.

Elaine is awake and, once she and Lucia have managed to pull her to a sitting position, she wants her wheelchair so she can go into the living room and watch television. With the toiletting, medicating, and various other kinds of necessary care, none of which Elaine can do for herself any more, and now the inane racket of the television set—Elaine's taste in programming is the same as a twelve-year-old's, although her dignity won't allow her to watch cartoons if Lucia is there—it will be late tonight before Lucia gets another chance to read.

Still, as she goes about her routine, she finds herself thinking about the book she's just finished. She tries to imagine herself in the author's shoes, her grandparents, aunts, uncles, cousins all dead—murdered, in fact—reduced from flesh to shadowy images in worn snapshots. But every time she feels herself getting close, the phone rings, or it's time for Elaine's medication, or the wash is ready for the dryer, or it's time to cook supper, and before long she's forgotten about the book.

Today they are in the waiting room two floors below ground level at Nuclear Medicine, Lucia sitting in a straight-backed chair beside Elaine's wheelchair until all the chairs are taken and she gives up hers to a newcomer. Then she leans against the wall next to Elaine under a sign warning of the presence of radioactive materials. Elaine is here to undergo tests that involve large machines, all steel, shiny chrome, and spotless white plastic, attached to banks of computer screens with flickering white graphs on blue backgrounds. They've seen these machines and computers as examination room doors open to let someone in or out, or else they know what they look like from television or movies, or maybe, Lucia thinks, they've seen them in their dreams.

The walls of this waiting room are a cream colour, the floors black-and-brown-speckled marble. The doors—extra wide to accommodate stretchers—are a pale wood, oak, perhaps, or maple. No, ash, Lucia decides. She doesn't actually know what ash looks like, it's just that ash seems the appropriate wood down here. She thinks she'll have to remember to tell George this the next time she manages a few days at home.

She glances around the room. People stare at the floor or gaze forward into space, the colourlessness of their eyes indicating that they see nothing, or perhaps it is a memory they've fallen into of some distant moment; the way the leaves in the yard crunched underfoot one fall day, maybe, or how the light used to stream through the bedroom window mornings when it was time to get up for school.

How shabby this room is, Lucia thinks. How dismal in its very shabby ordinariness. She thinks, If I were one of these dying people, what would I see if I looked? And in a visionary flash she sees how purely unendurable the thought of leaving even it behind must be.

This is more than even she, the non-dying, can bear. No one in this room is thinking what she's thinking, or they'd be on their knees, banging their heads against that marble floor, they'd be wailing and tearing their hair.

She drags herself back from this moment, some emotion well beyond mere pity forcing her to make another glance around the room at the men and women sitting in absent silence. She remembers the silly joke she cracked a few weeks earlier with her professor-friend and, annoyingly, tears rush to her eyes.

She has promised Elaine, on the evidence of a reply given

her by a nurse, that this time there'll be no needles, but when they've been waiting twenty minutes, they're called into a cubicle across the hall so that a technician can find one of Elaine's tiny veins and inject a radioactive fluid into it for the machines to pick out as it circulates through her blood. Elaine goes weekly for lab tests where blood is routinely drawn; she endures the chemotherapy needle and the finger pricks and the palpation of various lumps and sore spots. So far she's never protested, except for a whimper at the pain or, once in a while, an angry "ouch!"

Today, as the technician struggles to get his needle into a vein, she begins to cry. She sobs quietly, not protesting, not pulling her arm away, not asking Lucia to make the technician stop. She cries hopelessly, as if there will never be an end to this. Lucia holds Elaine's head pressed gently against her abdomen. The technician gives up, goes away, comes back with the department head who succeeds in hitting a vein on his first, extremely careful try.

She's into the first-person accounts now, one by a man and one by a woman. The male writer, about twelve at the time his family had been seized, had been lucky enough to stay with his father. He tells of how time and time again the father saves them both with his hard intelligence and a cunning that seems somehow able to cut through the trauma around him. The father never dwells on the monstrousness of what is going on, but instead he approaches the routine of each day with supreme but well-hidden alertness, always calculating what the best chances for their survival are in each situation. And he never takes his eyes off the day he knows will come when he and his son will escape or be freed. Nor does he ever forget, nor allow his son to forget, that outside these walls there is still a normal world to which they will return. When she's finished this book, Lucia thinks, I thought it would be so much worse than this to read.

The next night she begins the book by the woman. This memoirist can barely bring herself to tell her story. Every line—written, she says, only because her children say she must—is filled with an emotion deeper than mere sorrow or disgust or rage. There is no name for it in Lucia's vocabulary, but whatever it is, it is so deep and terrible that, thinking about it, Lucia can't see how the author has managed to live the fifty or more years since the events happened, and now, when she tells them.

It is with the woman that Lucia gets the sense of the daily horrors of camp life. Some images of Nazi cruelty she knows she will never be able to erase, and lying on the sagging, narrow little cot at night while Elaine sleeps fitfully, the condenser roaring, and sirens wailing down the street below, or the balcony doors rattling in sudden gusts of prairie wind, she tries to grasp some meaning out of this that she feels sure must be there beyond the general horror, the barely utterable cruelties, the awful suffering. Something moves in the darkness of her consciousness, well back from light. It is huge and, so far, shapeless. She doesn't know what it is, only that it isn't ready yet to come forward, to sweep her up into some new level of awareness. Or to madness, she thinks suddenly, when she sees it at last in its true form. Or perhaps in the end she will decide not to let it come forward into light. Perhaps she will have to turn away.

Elaine is not eating much now, and it's a chore to get her to drink anything. One eye has a slight infection, so added to the round of daily chores is the task of flushing it twice a day with a medicated fluid. Elaine tries to cooperate in this, but she blinks as the fluid falls from the eye dropper so that most of it trickles down her cheek.

"I'm sorry, Luce," she says, crying a little, and Lucia says, "If I were the one getting stuff poured into my eye, I'd blink too."

Elaine's nose is crusted and bloody inside from the irritation of the oxygen tubes constantly resting in it, which means nose drops and eventually antibiotics. The flesh between the oxygen tubing that hooks behind her ears and her skull grows more irritated and sore all the time, and Lucia and the home care nurse have had to devise padding that will stay in place there. Besides these small miseries, pains come and pains go, often in strange places, usually without explanation, as do other afflictions that can't be ignored: a rash, a swollen arm and hand, a swollen foot, a discharge, a painful shoulder, a painful hip. Each one requires phone calls to the home care staff, to the cancer clinic, to the family doctor.

Consultations take place, advice is given, then Lucia makes appointments at downtown laboratories for X-rays, or blood tests, or other, more complicated investigations. First, she has to order the wheelchair van since, as Elaine has grown weaker, Lucia can no longer get her in and out of her own car; then she has to take Elaine out for more waiting in other waiting rooms. In these, Elaine is always the sickest person present, and seeing this, the staff nearly always accelerates her admission into the inner sanctum. This is a kindness Lucia is always more grateful for than is Elaine who, falling into her peculiar waiting-room reverie, seems not to notice.

Over and over again Lucia has had to step outside these examination or treatment rooms and say softly to the attendant, "My sister is mildly mentally retarded, she does not understand what you are telling her," filled with shame for humiliating Elaine, irritation with the doctor, nurse, or technician's inability to see what appears to Lucia to be the obvious, and pity for Elaine. She finds herself, too, caught between guilt for betraying her sister, who is intelligent enough to know she doesn't think as well as other people and is permanently sick with disgust at herself because of it, and fear that the medical person she's talking to won't believe her, since in a brief, polite social exchange, Elaine simulates normal intelligence so well that no one would ever guess that she can't read or write.

Nothing much ever comes of these visits. If they reveal a new problem, it's always trivial in the light of the cancer, and if it's another symptom of the cancer's spread, there's nothing more that can be done than already is. Knowing all this in advance, or learning it as she goes along, Lucia has moments close to real despair, until she begins to view these usually weekly trips—in addition to the sometimes twice-weekly trips to the cancer clinic for various tests, examinations, and treatments, although they've given up on the chemotherapy—as outings for Elaine, a way of passing another day on the seemingly endless road to her demise.

George has given Lucia another survivor's story about her experience in the camp-village called Theresienstadt, and there's still the book about a Canadian Jewish committee's post-war struggle to find some Jewish orphans to bring to Canada. She spends a couple of hours on each, although neither does much more for her than to confirm what the memoirs have already seared into her brain. She puts them back without finishing them.

One night, she realizes she's finished the first stack of books. She moves to the second pile, which consists of the books that on George's advice she borrowed from the library. Elie Wiesel's *Night*, the thinnest of volumes, barely a hundred pages long, is on the top. Having seen him on television, and knowing him to be a Nobel Peace Prize winner, she's pretty sure this will be an exceptionally hard book to read. She hesitates while the electric clock on the wall above the table ticks erratically and the concentrator makes its breathy roar in the other room. After a moment she puts it back, crawls into her cot, and drifts into the state of semi-consciousness that these days passes for sleep.

She'd been home for the weekend. Five, or is it six, women have been involved in caring for Elaine over the three days she's been gone, an arrangement that took Lucia ten days to set up and then to ensure that the arrangements had gone down the full chain of command to the people who would actually be coming. More than once there's been some kind of bureaucratic foul-up at home care when Lucia, having made arrangements to go out to a hurried dinner with a friend, comes back to Elaine's apartment to find that the person who was supposed to make Elaine's supper hasn't shown up. Elaine is propped against the cushions on her couch just as Lucia had left her two or three hours earlier. Elaine is frightened beyond reason when this happens. According to the arrangements this time, Elaine should have been alone only for about an hour between the nurse's visit and Lucia's promised arrival by two.

She's driving up the three-mile-long avenue of fast-food restaurants, service stations, and motels that leads into the city. She's about halfway up it when she notices that so far she hasn't hit a single red light. Ordinarily it takes her as long as half an hour before she reaches the narrow side streets that lead to the apartment building where Elaine lives. There must be a dozen sets of traffic lights along this road, and not to have hit a single red one is so unusual she laughs out loud in surprise. Far ahead she sees another green light, almost brakes, thinking that by the time she reaches it, it will be red. But it stays green, and it stays green, and she sails right on through, and through the next one too, and then she knows. She knows absolutely that Elaine needs her. She puts her foot hard on the gas, knowing there'll be no red lights today, and in five minutes she's parking in front of Elaine's.

She finds her alone, instead of resting against the pillows, sitting forward on her couch, her forehead beaded with perspiration, her white face paler than Lucia has so far seen it no matter what atrocities are being done to her in various clinics around the city. Her lips, in this paste-white face, are blue. Her chest pumps in and out with a rapidity that appals Lucia; she can't begin to guess how many times a minute Elaine's chest is going in and out. Elaine stares at her with large, desperate eyes, barely able to speak.

"Where's the nurse?" Lucia asks stupidly.

"She ... left ..." Lucia tries to think what to do, runs into the bedroom and gathers the nebulizer—Elaine is supposed to use it twice a day but refuses to if Lucia isn't there to help her—the mask, the potent asthma-type drugs that the nebulizer converts to mist for Elaine to breathe in. Quickly she puts the drugs into their container, plugs in the nebulizer, pulls the mask up over her sister's mouth and nose. She takes Elaine's pulse as the machine whirrs away on Elaine's lap and the mask clouds with vapour and Elaine's head continues to bob with each breath. Her pulse is—Lucia almost can't believe it—150 beats a minute. The phone sits on the sofa beside Elaine and now Lucia dials the home care nurse's mobile phone.

"Call an ambulance," the nurse tells her. "Don't wait. Call an ambulance. Here, I'll give you the number."

She copies down the number, but Lucia finds herself reluctant to dial it, Elaine hates hospitals so, but she can't imagine now what will happen if she doesn't obey—how long can Elaine go on gasping this way before—she doesn't know what, only that surely Elaine will die. She dials, and in less than ten minutes, during which time Elaine continues to pant, her torso jerking and her head bobbing with every breath as she struggles for air, three ambulance attendants, a stretcher, and some bulky equipment have taken up all the available space in the small living room.

"She had polio as a child," she tells the attendants, just as she has had to tell everyone in every clinic and waiting room and doctor's office through this whole odyssey, because no one ever seems to realize that Elaine can't walk. "You'll have to lift her."

The ambulance attendants, all young men, are kind, and gentle, and reassuring. Stethoscopes appear, and various other medical paraphernalia which Elaine can't recall later, but she remembers a hypodermic syringe and vials of medication. They change Elaine's oxygen supply to the portable tank they've brought with them. In mere minutes they have Elaine half sitting on the stretcher and are wheeling her out of the apartment, Lucia reassuring her, "Don't worry, I'll be right behind you. I'll be at the hospital as soon as you are." Elaine continues to gasp for breath with her whole frame as the elevator doors close on the stretcher.

Lucia beats the ambulance to the hospital. Nobody is more surprised by this than her, she can only be grateful she wasn't stopped for speeding, and when the ambulance does arrive nearly ten minutes later, it remains parked next to the Emergency entrance, motor running, for another ten minutes with nobody emerging. She waits, pacing, not daring to knock on the ambulance doors, afraid of what's happening on the other side of them.

Finally they open and her sister's stretcher is lowered and wheeled into the hospital through doors Lucia isn't allowed to pass through. When she rushes inside and asks if she may go into the treatment room, she's told, absolutely not, and it looks as if the receptionist / nurse telling her this wouldn't hesitate to wrestle her to the ground if she shows the slightest sign of disobeying.

Moments pass, she paces, staring through the double doors, the top half of which are glass, into the suite of rooms where her sister has vanished.

"You can go in now," somebody tells her. She finds Elaine in the room next to the nursing station, seated nearly upright in what looks like an old-fashioned dentist's chair. At least six doctors, nurses, and technicians surround her, each of them doing something to Elaine, although Lucia, in her confusion, can't make any sense of the scene, except to relax a little because her sister is in good hands. A man in operating-room greens, his mask dangling from a string, detaches himself from the scrum around Elaine and introduces himself as doctor somebody. He questions her about Elaine's diagnosis, her condition, and repeats in a casual way some of her answers to the crowd around Elaine.

Before too long Lucia sees someone else being rushed past on a stretcher into the room next door to Elaine's and most of the people clustered around Elaine abruptly leave. She hears orders being given, she hears the new patient moaning, she sees nurses rushing out and then in again. Listening, Lucia hears the unmistakable sounds, which she knows from watching television hospital dramas, of someone dying and being brought back to life. Twice, she hears this. Her abdomen and chest feel hollow. She's not sure she's breathing, although she must be, but if she is, it seems she isn't getting any air. Elaine is drowsy now. Lucia kisses her cheek, gets her a paper cup of icy water, murmurs softly whatever comforting words come to her.

Elaine is breathing less quickly now, although when Lucia surreptitiously takes her pulse, it's still over a hundred beats a minute. It occurs to her to wonder why Pierre Trudeau didn't make time metric too, but then she thinks, maybe it already is. How bizarre these thoughts are doesn't occur to her until months later. Nurses return and try again to insert a line into Elaine's vein and Elaine cries and behaves like a frightened child and one of the nurses snaps at her. Once more Lucia has to explain why Elaine is hospital-and-needle phobic.

It is because of the polio when she was five years old, when she nearly died in the old wing of this very hospital, according to their mother, screaming with pain for days and nights on end until the head nurse told their parents Elaine would not live through another night. Then she was kept here for more than seven months in isolation, with two dozen other children, living as if they were all orphans. She summarizes the surgeries, each one more horrible than the last. Lucia has to do this in such a way that Elaine does not hear that she is not as smart as other people, that in some ways she remains a child still, while the nurses do hear Lucia's message.

Hours later, while Elaine sleeps on a ward in the hospital, Lucia drives through the summer twilight to her sister's apartment. She remembers how earlier she'd careened around corners, sped down residential streets, and screeched to stops at traffic lights, only to arrive ten minutes ahead of the ambulance. She's been told now, or rather, since nobody ever tells her anything she considers meaningful, she's figured out that her sister has narrowly escaped death. If Lucia hadn't hit all those green lights on the way into town, she might have found Elaine's corpse. And she realizes that the paramedics had tried and failed to find a vein while Elaine was on her way to the hospital. Now she thinks that maybe that's why the driver went slowly, so as not to jolt the paramedic struggling with Elaine's damaged veins, and why they'd taken so long to open the ambulance doors.

Alone in Elaine's apartment, she picks up Wiesel's *Night*

again. This time she opens it to the first page and begins reading. At first she forces herself, then, although she wants to stop, she gets caught up in the harrowing narrative and can't. She reads, her gut in knots, her palms wet with sweat, her breathing shallow and fast, as if she is perhaps asleep and dreaming some intense, frightening dream. She feels as though she's caught in the throes of some terminal disease whose symptoms are amazement, horror, disgust, and an unfathomably deep shock that the world could, after all, contain such depths of savagery, such depths of suffering. When, hours later, she finishes the book, she sits on the side of her cot for a long time staring into space.

After a while she wanders to the balcony doors to gaze out over the concrete-grey of the city, tinged purple in the bleak light of the powerful street lamps. She thinks about Elie Wiesel, about a certain expression that appears on his face when she's seen him being interviewed on television. She doesn't think she's seen it on anyone else's face, and every time she's seen it on his, she's wondered what it means.

She thinks she understands it now. Since the camps he has become a witness, determined never to look away from the terrible pictures he carries in his mind, or from the stories he's been told, the photographs he's seen.

For once, the streets outside the apartment are quiet, no drunken young people shouting, nobody roaring his motor or squealing his tires on the road leading onto the bridge that crosses the wide river, no fire trucks or ambulances or police cars screaming past where she stands alone in her nightgown in the shadows. She stares up at the moon hanging hard and white over the city, and thinks of all the millennia it has been shining down on this planet. For a moment, the belief she's been taught, that every single human death matters, wavers and almost disappears.

The world does not make sense, she thinks. One horror ends and somewhere another is beginning. She must not look away either, she tells herself, but doubts she has the courage to carry out such a resolve.

After Elaine's return from her week-long stay in the hospital, her needs grow in quantity and intensity. Since they can't afford to hire a professional nurse to stay with her—only the rich could do that—the visits from home care attendants and nurses increase. Elaine's case manager drops in, drinks coffee with them, chats in a friendly way. She's here to assess the situation: both Lucia and Elaine know that soon, if she doesn't die first, Elaine will have to go to a facility equipped to care for someone as ill as she is, maybe even to a palliative care unit in a hospital. When Lucia hasn't the strength to lift her out of bed one more time, to leap up from sleep one more time to rush into her room and pull her up in bed, even then, she can't imagine how they will get Elaine to consent to go.

Lucia has lost quite a lot of weight, she has chronic diarrhea now and a number of random aches and pains which she tries to ignore, but which, nonetheless, alarm her. She wants to go home, she wants to lie down and sleep for a month, she wants George to come and hold her. One day someone phones to tell her that the friend she ran into at the cancer clinic so long ago, and to whom she made that stupid, unfunny joke, has died.

Now Elaine is staying alive on oxygen and morphine and an unwillingness to die. Lucia has begun to wish the end would come, the quicker the better, and she finds herself irritated with Elaine's refusal to face what is happening to her. Early on, when Elaine had misunderstood a doctor's message to her, taking it as hopeful when it was really a statement of hopelessness, and Lucia had tried gently to correct her misunderstanding, Elaine had screamed, "I'm sick and tired of you telling me

I'm going to die!" Now Lucia can't bring herself to try to talk to Elaine about her impending death, and she hates herself for her desire, which she can no longer deny, that Elaine should give up this fight she can't win.

She's read all the books in the stacks behind the kitchen door now, or all that she can bear to read; there is only a work by Primo Levi left that she's determined to try. Primo Levi comes highly recommended from a rabbi-professor friend of George's, and so she places his book on the top of the pile to begin reading once Elaine has had her evening morphine and for a few hours will be unconscious. Although it seems to her she's done what she set out to do, however unclear that intention was and, in some ways, remains, her new knowledge has not brought her peace, or any new understanding, or even any satisfaction. She doesn't know what it is she wants, but whatever it is, it hasn't yet come. Maybe it never will, maybe she isn't wise enough or smart enough. Maybe she's too weak. Or maybe she has to be the victim, instead of just a helper, to know what it is.

Evenings now, after the last visit from the palliative care nurse, and the last home care helper has long since departed, Lucia spends a lot of time on the phone. Relatives call from across the country, there's her evening talk with George, sometimes the family doctor calls, or a friend or two. It's quite late before she's able to make up her cot, undress for bed, and climb in with her book. Since she learned how as a six-year-old, to read before sleep has been her habit, and now, despite her exhaustion, she clings to it as the only remnant of normalcy left in her life.

Levi's book is a careful, scholarly dissection of the degrees, causes, and purposes of specific daily cruelties in the concentration camps of the Second World War. It examines in detail, coldly, human evil as it manifests itself in the simplest and smallest of everyday acts. This book is the worst of them all, and she's read only a few pages before she begins to wonder if she can go on.

Elaine has begun to cough. Lucia throws back her blanket and sheet and hurries into the bedroom. Surprisingly, given that she is now constantly heavily drugged with morphine, Elaine is awake. Her blue eyes, grown large and beautiful in these last weeks, shine in the semi-dark, and through her spasms of coughing she tries to speak to Lucia.

"Yes, okay," Lucia murmurs, although she hasn't been able to understand her sister's broken mumbling. She tries, using her usual techniques, to partly pull, partly lift Elaine back up to a sitting position, but for some reason it is one of those nights when she can't manage it. Maybe it's because Elaine can't help her any more by pushing against the mattress with her hands.

Frantically, she climbs onto the bed beside Elaine and puts one arm against her back to hold her up. Elaine's cough has settled into a steady, gasping roll that is terrifying to hear. Lucia reaches with her other arm for the pillows and the foam wedge to pull them down to where she's holding Elaine up in her sitting position, but she can't get a grip on them, and when she does, the wedge refuses to move, seems to be caught on something she can't see or reach. Elaine is trying to speak again. Lucia freezes.

"I'm … so … scared …" Panic grips Lucia, her helplessness, her desire to save her sister any suffering she can, her hopeless, endless failure to do so, and the demands of the moment that she can't even consider rush through her mind. She tries, but from here she can't reach the phone without letting go of Elaine and she doesn't dare do that.

Upright now, Elaine's coughing has subsided enough that Lucia can feel her short gasping breaths returning to shudder through her chest and ribs and spine.

"I'm ... so ... tired ... I ... need ... sleep ..." Elaine whispers: a word, a breath, a word, a breath. Lucia gives up the struggle to pull the wedge and pillows to her. Holding Elaine upright with her left arm, on all fours she moves around behind her, transfers Elaine's weight to her left shoulder, while she tugs at and straightens her own nightgown that has twisted around her legs. Then she crouches behind Elaine, her face hovering level with the back of her sister's stubbly head. Slowly she lowers herself until she's seated behind her.

She spreads her legs so that they enclose Elaine, and the pillows and wedge fit her own back, neatly propping her upright. She puts both arms around Elaine, pulls up the sheet and blankets, pats them into place, folding them down under Elaine's chin. Then she clasps her hands on Elaine's lap, and accepts her sister's full weight, surprisingly heavy for all her thinness, her frailty, against her chest and abdomen and thighs.

Elaine falls back into unconsciousness almost immediately, her head lolling against Lucia's throat, chin, and shoulder. The concentrator drones on beside the bed and the city's light glows in around the curtains so that Lucia can make out the shadows that are furniture. Slowly her sister's twisted, knobby spine relaxes and settles into the warm cushion of Lucia's breasts and belly.

Lucia's mind wanders to the book by Primo Levi she's been trying to read, she remembers reading that Levi committed suicide. She grasps Elaine more firmly, presses her lips lightly against her sister's clammy cheek. She thinks of their parents, dead now, and of her and Elaine's long childhood together in the bright, quivering aspen forests of the north, of the moving sky there, the intense green of the grass.

Elaine coughs, a light, shallow cough, moves her head slightly, her short, stiff hair brushing Lucia's mouth, before she relaxes again against Lucia's warm body.

They stay that way a long time, Elaine deeply unconscious, her polio-and-pain-stiffened shoulders, neck, and back slowly loosening so that they feel almost normal to Lucia, while Lucia drifts in and out of sleep, until the heat of their two bodies has so melded that, awake now as the first pale rays of dawn seep around the drawn curtains, Lucia can no longer tell where her sister leaves off and she begins.

Winterkill

"Pammy! Get a move on." There was no answer, but feet began thumping down the stairs. Without turning around Bonny called, "Where's Jason?" The radio was playing softly beside the sink and she reached with a soapy hand to shut it off.

"An aboriginal man claims that he'd been driven by the police to the outskirts of the city Thursday night, and left to walk back—" She pulled her hand back, soap bubbles sliding from her wrist onto the counter.

"I dunno," Pam answered in a singsong voice, always happiest before figure-skating practice. "Com-ing, I guess."

"He says that the policemen also took his jacket. It was forty below that night. He says that he pounded on the door of the power plant until the night watchman—"

She could tell by the muffled thuds and exclamations that Jason was at the back door now, too. Pam had stopped humming and the two of them were into the did-not-did-too-did-not quarrelling they seemed to do in their sleep, but which had been especially bad this winter with Ross gone from the farm all week.

"Cut that out!" Bonny shouted, moving her head closer to

the radio. "Police say they are looking into the freezing deaths of two aboriginal men whose bodies were found on the outskirts of the city near the Queen Elizabeth power plant. Aboriginal leaders—"

She could see through the window above her sink that already the shadows were growing longer, turning the shining hills a mile away across the snow-covered stubble field a deep blue. Such a cold January, a record breaker. She remembered the sink, pulled the plug, and let the water drain. The radio was still playing, but she couldn't make sense of what the announcer was saying, and after a pause, during which she held her hand an inch from the knob, listening and frowning, she snapped it off.

She dried her hands rapidly on the tea towel, went to the back door, and pulled on her boots and parka to run outside and start the truck so it would warm up before she drove them into town. Jason had his snowpants and boots on, and was searching for something in his hockey bag. Pammy was rubbing intently with a moistened finger at a spot on the boot of one skate. Too bad Ross would miss Jason's game, but there was no help for it. Without his job they couldn't pay their bills; without her part-time work at the nursing home, they couldn't even buy groceries.

Her boots squeaked on the packed snow as she hurried across the yard to the shed that in winter housed the truck. She held one mittened hand over her mouth as she ran; the air was too cold to breathe it in directly. She couldn't get the block-heater plug to separate from its connection, had to pull off a mitt for a better grip, and her fingers stung where they touched the freezing metal. There was no place at the rink in town to plug vehicles in and she worried that she'd have to let the truck run during Pam's practice and Jason's game. But with the price of gas—I'll just have to go out and start it every half-hour or so, she decided.

What a nuisance—but it was the only way to keep the motor warm so the truck would start when it was time to go home. Now, even plugged in and in the shed, the motor turned over reluctantly and, huddled and shivering behind the wheel, she had to keep playing the gas pedal until it was running smoothly.

Thank God, Ross would be home in the morning. His being away all week was part of what made the winter so long; at least he didn't leave me with animals to look after, and before she could squelch it, maybe next year we should all move to Swift Current for the winter; then, no, better to wish our bills were paid so none of us have to go to Swift Current. This reminded her of the mail waiting in the drawer for Ross to deal with. There was an envelope from the bank, probably another statement; she never opened the ones from the bank, and dreaded the moment when Ross did.

The older boys were just finishing cleaning the ice as the three of them made their way into the rink. Jason immediately dumped his hockey equipment on the bleachers and hurried back to the lobby with a few boys from his team to play a noisy game of tag until the girls' practice was over and their game would start. As he ran away, Bonny called to him, "Stay out of trouble," as much for the benefit of any adults around as because she thought Jason, who, thank heaven, wasn't a problem kid, might get into something he wasn't supposed to. She finished lacing Pam's skates and went to join the other mothers where they sat snuggled together on the wooden benches. Pam skated out to join the other girls who crowded around their teacher and her assistant at centre ice. It was much colder than usual in the rink, and instead of their usual practice outfits of very short skirts and tights, most of the girls were wearing heavy sweatpants or ski-pants and light jackets.

"Ross back yet?" Colleen asked.

"Tomorrow morning. He's working too late tonight to come back." Rita and Irene arrived, every breath making small white clouds, and the line of seated women slid down to make room for them.

"Brrrr, it's cold," Irene said, taking off her glasses and using her thumbnail to scrape off the frost that had formed on them. The others mumbled agreement. On the ice the girls had divided into four groups, each group skating off to a corner. The club's star, Tammy Jo, was practising spins at the blue line on the women's left. Pam's group had gone to Bonny's right on the far side of the ice. There they had joined hands and were skating in a circle, halting, and skating back the other way, trying, but mostly failing, to keep synchronized. With the carnival only a couple of weeks away, they'd have to keep at it until they had it right. Pam's group's skating was still jerky, lacked the grace of the older girls, except for Pam who was a little sprite on skates and, as usual, led them as they snaked out of the circle, reversed in synch, and stopped in a wavy line that was supposed to be straight, the little one on the end stumbling and almost falling.

Bonny was about to ask Colleen about the home-and-school meeting when she noticed that Denise McKenzie, carrying her baby bundled in blankets and her toddler at her side, had entered the rink near where Pam and the other girls were practising, and stood watching them. Bonny said, nodding her head in Denise's direction and laughing, "She's getting that little one started early."

Colleen said loudly, "It's too cold for her to be out with that baby! She's not a month old!" Irene, using the same disapproving tone, said, "I saw her at the bake sale on Tuesday and she put that baby on the bake sale table and changed her diaper! Can you imagine?"

"In the grocery store?" Bonny asked. "Where else would she put her? On the floor?"

"Such a bad mother," Annette said sternly, puffs of white spurting with each word. Bonny had been about to point out how Denise took her children with her everywhere and the baby never fussed and the toddler didn't run around like a little maniac as most of the other kids did. How Denise spoke quietly to them, her voice full of warmth, not screaming like the other mothers so often did. But now the rest of the women were joining in, and the conversation went on around her, all of it negative, while Denise stood on the other side of the rink watching the girls falling down and getting up again, oblivious to the fact that she was the object of such nastiness. Bonny gave up trying to defend her, or even listening, and transferred her attention to Pam.

It was after eight when she turned the key in the ignition and after a few seconds of growling the engine putted, then rumbled into life. She'd insisted that Ross take the newer truck to work, he'd offered to leave her the better one, but she knew men and their vehicles. They felt shamed if they had to drive an old clunker, it was worse if everybody knew you had money trouble, and she didn't want Ross going through that. But nobody remarked on it if the women drove the clunkers— most of the staff at work did.

They rode in silence, the two children tired and beginning to drowse. The coach hadn't played Jason much, but as long as Ross wasn't there to see it, Jason didn't care. Now, as if he knew she'd been thinking about him, he stirred, and asked in his high voice, "Mom, what happens when you freeze to death?" Startled, she turned to him. Had he heard that report on the radio? Had the kids been talking about it?

"Nothing happens, sweetie," she said. "You just go to sleep. You don't feel a thing."

"Oh," Jason said. After a moment, he said, "But, Mom, when

I stay out too long and my toes get cold, they *hurt*—they hurt a lot." Bonny said, "But you couldn't feel your nose that time when you froze the end, could you?"

The heater kept only the centre of the windshield ice-free, she had to lean forward to see out, and even in her heavy boots her toes were stinging with cold. The kids sat huddled against each other to keep warm, despite the blanket she'd insisted they keep over their legs. She thought, I shouldn't have taken them out in this cold, but knew that if Jason had missed the game, Ross would have been angry. Ross thought that Jason was NHL material, that any day now his natural talent would surface. Ross's attitude made Bonny despair since it seemed clear to everybody else that Jason had no talent, and besides, didn't really like hockey, was far too dreamy a kid for such rough-and-tumble stuff, would rather be at home reading a book or watching television.

Pam was the one with the talent. But whenever she pointed out how quickly Pam learned the figures, how easy it all was for her, Ross would agree, then promptly forget or discount it. Figure-skating lessons weren't cheap, although cheaper than hockey, another thing that she couldn't get Ross to see, and she just prayed she could get enough shifts at the nursing home—the care centre, she was supposed to call it—to keep Pam enrolled, since if there wasn't enough money, it would be Pam who would have to quit.

They were pulling into the yard when Pammy said, "Look! the lights are on—Daddy's home!"

"Yay!" Jason shouted, wide awake now.

Ross was in the kitchen, heating a plate of leftovers in the microwave. He hugged the kids, asked Jason how his hockey game had gone.

"We lost," Jason told him, studying the floor.

"What are you doing back so soon?" Bonny asked quickly,

kissing Ross's lean, bristly cheek. He'd gotten thin over the winter and it worried her. He peered into the microwave.

"The truck I was supposed to work on didn't come in. Too cold, I guess. So I came home."

"I'll make coffee," she told him, reaching for the pot with fingers still stiff from the cold. The kids sat at the table, one on each side of Ross as he ate, and chattered away to him, and she leaned against the counter, listening, while she waited for the coffee to finish dripping through its filter.

"Your mother has invited us for supper tomorrow night," she told him, keeping her voice neutral.

"Oh, yeah?" he said, then, glancing up at her, "We won't stay late."

Later, after the kids were asleep, and she and Ross had gone to bed, made love, and now were lying together talking softly, she said, "Honey, do you think that next year we should maybe all go to Swift Current for the winter? I mean, so we wouldn't have to be apart?"

"No!" he said, too quickly. "We've been over this and over it. You know I can stay with Uncle George and Aunt Rose for nothing, but we can't all do that. We can't afford to rent a place, besides, it would look to everybody like we'd given up."

"It's just so lonesome without you," she said. "And you're missing Jason's games and the ice carnival is coming up—"

"If we get a crop this year," he said, "next winter I can stay home."

"We've got enough snow," she said. "There should be lots of runoff—"

"It's too early to tell—it could all go in one February chinook." This was too pessimistic, but she said nothing, knowing he wasn't really talking to her. "I figure by the end of March I should clear maybe twelve thousand—"

"Where will we put it?"

"Jeeze," Ross said, taking his arm out from under her neck, and moving to a half-sitting position, "on the way home I was figuring and figuring. There's last year's taxes, there's the tractor payment, there's the fuel bill and the chemical bill—Steve won't wait for his chemical payment—"

Bonny said, "Let's not talk about it. It doesn't do any good and we should get some sleep."

"Taxes first. We've got to hang onto the land—what's left of it." Last fall the bank had seized a quarter section. In the darkness she fumbled for his hand and grasped it in both her own.

"If they take the tractor, we're sunk too," she said. His hand lay limp in hers, as if he hadn't noticed she'd touched him.

"Chickpeas," he was saying. "It's the only crop that's paying right now—"

"But the seed, I hear it's really expensive—" She'd let go of his hand and pushed her pillow up so that she was half sitting up as well.

"I'd only seed maybe eighty acres. Or only fifty. You got to treat the land first, fifteen bucks an acre for chemical, and Steve won't give me any more credit—"

"Maybe try the Pool?"

"I'll ask Uncle George for a loan. I know he'd give it to me. Give him a share of the crop."

"If we get a crop."

"Crop insurance covers good on chickpeas."

"Really?" She felt a little stir of hope. "Sounds like the way to go then," and slid over against his warm body. Then she remembered the envelope in the drawer in the kitchen, and her little kernel of hope quivered and vanished.

When they drove into Ross's mother's yard they saw that Audrey, Ross's sister, and her husband Dwayne and their kids had already arrived. As they made their way into the house Bonny steeled herself.

"Ross!" his mother said, as eagerly, Bonny thought, as if he'd been away with the French Foreign Legion. She hugged her son, then her grandchildren, and finally, her tone changing, greeted Bonny.

"Hi, Ruth," Bonny answered. "I brought a jar of my straw-berries." She knew better than to try to hand them directly to Ruth, who would turn away from Bonny's outstretched hand as if she hadn't noticed, leaving her standing there with the jar thrust into empty space.

"I always freeze any extras," her mother-in-law told her. "They taste better than the canned ones." Bonny repressed a sigh. And yet, if she showed up with nothing, Ross would hear how bad-mannered she was.

The kids had gone to the basement rec room to play with their older cousins. She could hear Max, her father-in-law, booming about the coldness of the winter to Ross in the living room, and she hoped he'd stay off the topic of their money situation. Ross's dad mustn't know Ross was going to borrow money from Max's older brother. He had none left to give them himself, and Max would be furious if he thought his brother knew this. She pitied Ross: Max made it a regular prac-tice to remind him what an incompetent he was for being in financial trouble. Never mind that it didn't have anything to do with Ross's skill as a farmer, or with bad decisions, or that they spent money like drunken sailors as he sometimes accused them. Max knew perfectly well everybody was in trouble.

She followed Ruth and Audrey into the kitchen. In the first year of her marriage, whenever she'd gone into the kitchen and said politely, "Can I help?" meaning, to get the meal on the table or to clean up and wash the dishes, her sister-in-law and mother-in-law would say, "Oh, we're okay," not meeting her eyes, deliberately leaving her to stand there doing nothing while they worked and chatted to each other. It was unheard of to go sit in the living room with the men. Finally, she'd stopped offering, had begun joining them in the work without asking. At first they'd tried to ignore her, but eventually even that dropped away. Bonny saw this, glumly, as her only victory.

At dinner, feigning interest, she asked Audrey, "How are Jade and Ellen doing?" Jade was at university in Regina and Ellen in nursing in Calgary.

"Oh, good, really good," Audrey replied. "Ellen's in pediatrics right now and she really likes it. She always was good with kids." Ellen, picking up on her mother's disapproval of Bonny, used to tease Pam and Jason until they cried and one of the adults had to intervene.

"Nursing is a good profession," Bonny murmured noncommittally, accepting the bowl of steaming carrots.

"There's such a shortage," Audrey said. "They have to work such long hours and they get treated so badly, on their feet all the time ..."

For the first few years of her marriage Bonny had smiled all the time when she was with Ross's family, and had agreed with everything either her mother-in-law or sister-in-law said, until she saw that whenever she agreed with them, they would promptly switch sides as Audrey had just done. While she poured gravy over his potatoes, making sure Jason didn't spill anything on Ruth's tablecloth or she'd never hear the end of it, she was thinking, Why did you tell her to go into nursing then? Why are you so proud that she's going to be a nurse? There would soon be a dig at her, who could only work as a housekeeper at the nursing home, not having gone to nursing school.

"Yes," Audrey finished. "If she's going to work in a hospital, at least she's a nurse and not down on her hands and knees scrubbing the hospital floors." She dug vigorously into her slice of roast beef, sawing away, as if she didn't hear the sudden silence that had fallen over the table. Bonny wanted to say, It was your brother got me pregnant when I was only eighteen so I couldn't go to nursing school. But they all believed she'd trapped Ross, instead of the other way around, Ross pursuing her until she'd begun to fall for him. Not that she had a second's regret about marrying him—except for his family, that is.

The worst of it was that Ross seemed oblivious. When she complained he would say, "Aw, Bonny, she didn't mean anything," implying that this was only the silly squabbling of women that men could safely ignore. It was the one incurable in their marriage, which after years of quarrels that had grown steadily worse, by mutual agreement, they now avoided ever mentioning.

But riding home in the freezing darkness, Jason asleep on her lap and Pammy against Ross's shoulder, she said, "I can't understand why they're so mean to me." Ross let air out through his lips noisily, turned his head away from her and then back again, but didn't speak. "I mean, you'd think they'd be happy that you found a wife who takes good care of the kids and looks after you and …" Her voice trailed away. "They just don't seem to know how to stop," she said, puzzled. "Like their meanness just got away on them."

Ross still didn't say anything, and she forced herself not to go on. Instead of speaking, she lifted her hand to scrape away a patch of frost from her window so that she could peer out. It was forty below now, even the newer truck they were riding in creaked and groaned against the cold, the tires squeaking on the road so cold that it wasn't even slippery any more. There was no moon, the sky was dark as ink and full of stars, even the most distant ones that you never saw otherwise showing up with a faint silver light.

"Did you hear about the Native men they found frozen to death in Saskatoon?" she asked.

"Yeah," he said. "Drunk, I guess. Or doped up on drugs."

"Didn't you hear?" she asked, surprised. "The radio said that two policemen had taken them out to the country and left them to freeze to death—they even took their jackets. At least, that's what they're accused of doing."

"Do you believe that?" he asked, as if he found her naivete amusing.

"Don't you?" She could feel him shrug. "Jason keeps asking me about it," she told him. "Tonight when I went to the bathroom he caught up to me in the hall and asked me why the policemen did it. His eyes—" She stopped. "I told him it's probably not even true." She'd bent and held Jason tight against her chest.

"I'll sure be glad when this cold spell ends," Ross said. "I should have a talk with Art about playing Jason more." Now it was her turn to turn her head away from him in exasperation. Poor Jason, she thought, and would have tried one more time to persuade Ross that Jason wasn't very good as a hockey player, but gave it up before she began—it never did the slightest good. Casting about for something to say that would be on neutral ground, she told him about the women and Denise McKenzie at the rink on Friday night.

"I can't figure out why they pick on her," she said. "She seems nice to me—at least as nice as they are—and she keeps the kids clean and nobody ever said she's a bad housekeeper—"

"Women gossip," he said, as if this was something she ought to know without him having to tell her. She wanted to protest that the men were just as bad—what about coffee row—but once more held her tongue. They rode the next couple of miles before Ross broke the silence. "We've got this guy at work, Winston. Not too smart. The boss gets half his wages paid by the government. He sweeps the shop floor, takes out the garbage, washes parts—that kind of thing."

"Oh? Can he do the work?"

"Sure," Ross said. "It's all stuff you don't have to be smart to do. Hell, he's so eager it's pathetic." A kind of growl had entered his tone.

"Oh," she said, understanding, "and the men tease him."

"One especially," Ross said. "Won't leave him alone. Made him cry yesterday." She waited, knowing he was holding something back. "That's the real reason I came home last night. I told the boss if he didn't do something about the way Chuck is always after Winston, I'd do something myself. Then I walked out, came home. I'll be lucky if I'm not fired."

"You did the right thing," she assured him.

"It won't be so right if I don't have a job."

For a second a chill of sheer terror entered Bonny's heart: they'd lose the farm, they'd have nothing to eat; there was still the envelope from the bank to be opened.

"I don't care," she said, through clenched teeth. "It was still right." Jason stirred and she cupped her hand over his cold cheek. She wondered suddenly if Pammy were really asleep or just pretending.

Bonny woke, thinking, Sunday morning, too cold to go to church, and was glad that today they'd all be together at home. Tomorrow morning Ross would be gone by six in order to be at work by eight. She put her hand out to touch him and encountered only a wrinkled sheet, then remembered that Sunday morning was when he looked at the week's mail, and she threw back the covers, got up quickly, sliding her feet into her slippers and pulling on her robe.

In the kitchen, Ross had started the coffee and the radio on the counter was playing softly. He was seated in his usual place at the end of the table, his back slumped, his elbows resting on the table, his head in his hands. The opened mail sat in a pile in front of him. She went straight to him, put her hands gently on his shoulders, and bent to rest her cheek for a moment on the top of his head. He didn't respond, she could feel an odd current running through him as if all his muscles were tightened, ready to spring, and straightening, she saw that he was staring down at the letter from the bank. He moved his hand as if to tell her to read it.

"What does it say?"

"They're taking another quarter." Bonny gasped. "I was going to plant chickpeas on that quarter," he said, turning to look up at her, his voice plaintive as a child's.

She pulled out a chair to sit beside him as, at the same moment, he rose abruptly, his chair scraping backward with a harsh squeal.

"Jesus Christ!" He picked the chair up by its back and threw it across the kitchen where it came to rest, upright, against the far wall. "Goddamn—" He grabbed the chair that sat by the door leading into the hall and threw it, too. It struck the wall by the back door, bounced off, and skittered on its side across the well-polished vinyl floor back toward his feet. Bonny jumped up.

"Ross! The kids!" She hurried to the door into the hall and closed it quietly. Ross gripped the waist-high counter with both hands, facing the cupboards, his shoulders raised awkwardly. She reached out to touch his rigid back, but he released his hold on the counter and pushed her hand away roughly. She stood quietly for a moment, waiting for him to break down, to begin to cry, but instead he spun away from her and kicked the chair that lay on its side on the floor. Bonny backed away, went back to the table, and sat down where she'd been before, her back to him. She could hear him beginning to pace, taking long strides, kicking the chair away again and again, cursing under his breath.

She would wait until he'd calmed down and then she'd start making suggestions: Talk to the banker; tell him we'll plant chickpeas so we can pay some of our debt. See if the Pool will give us more credit. She tried frantically to think of other possibilities. Behind her, Ross was still pacing, although he'd stopped kicking the chair every time he passed it.

"Can't they *see* how much they need us?" he asked. His voice had gone high; it vibrated with tension. "Why are they *doing* this to us? Why doesn't the government *do* something?" She didn't try to answer him—nobody knew the answer to those questions, except that it seemed that the wealthy and powerful, whoever they were, wherever they were, cared only for their own wealth and power, and spared no thought for the people whose lives they destroyed.

Now Ross began telling her his plans—already he'd begun to make the plans that would surely save them—but she knew what he would say before he said it, having thought of all these things herself.

"Listen, Ross," she said. Her voice reminded her of the school principal both she and Ross had once had, and hated, but she didn't try to modulate it. *"Listen to me!"* He stopped pacing and she turned to face him. He was gazing at her out of eyes that, dark as they were, blazed, but in a way that struck her with fear, although not for herself. She almost faltered, but caught herself in time and went ahead anyway, even as she knew what she had to say would be futile, that in his outrage and his refusal to face that they were done, finished, he might even strike her.

"We should put the farm up for sale right now," she told him. "Just keep the home quarter while we make our plans to leave.

We'll go to the city—you're a good mechanic, you can get a good job." Ross took a step backward, not taking his eyes off her face, but she could see the colour leaching out of his cheeks and forehead. "Listen, Ross," she said again, urgently. "Listen to me. I'll go back to school, get a nurse's aide certificate so I can get a proper job. We can wait till fall to move so the kids can start the year in their new school." Ross had backed away as she spoke; he was at the back door, pushing his feet into his boots now, reaching for his parka. She raised her voice, calling to him to listen to her, "Summer holidays we can come back here to the house—"

Ross had to shove hard to get the back door opened, ice crackling away from it and falling to shatter on the packed snow on the cement steps. He slammed the door shut, leaving her standing alone in the kitchen. Once again she listened to him scurrying across the yard. She could hear the truck door creak open, then slam shut, in the icy morning silence she could even hear the ignition grinding as he tried to get the truck started. Finally, the motor came to life and he began to back the truck out of the yard, stalling it, he hadn't let the motor warm up long enough, and starting it again. Then she heard him drive away.

Despite his hard slam, the door hadn't closed. Feeling the draft of cold air seep in, she tried to shut it properly. She bent to shove away the broken stalactites of ice that burned when her fingers touched them, and the rigid ice frame that had been dislodged when he forced the door open now fell partly into the kitchen, preventing the door from closing. The tips of her fingers ached with the cold and began to turn blue. Out of habit she glanced at the outdoor thermometer that was fixed to the wall and saw that during the night it had grown even colder; this morning it was fifty below. At last she was able to shut the door tightly. She backed away from the rush of billowing white condensation that hung around the closed door.

She picked up the chairs that Ross had thrown and set them back in their places at the table. Then she sat down on one of them and stared out the window into the darkness. It wouldn't be daylight for at least another hour and when the sun rose, gleaming, palely-tinted mirages of fields of snow and distant, ephemeral villages would hover above the horizon all the way into town.

How cold it was, nothing moved out there, even the deer would freeze, and the cruelty of this for a moment made her mind go blank. She thought of the aboriginal men who had frozen to death on that country road in view of the lights of the city. In her mind she saw one of them as he began to walk. He would know he couldn't make it back to town before the cold killed him, and that on a night like this, no one would be driving down this isolated road and rescue him.

His teeth would begin to chatter, maybe he would run anyway, trying to keep his blood flowing, but then his lungs would burn from the frigid, ice-crystal-laden air and the pain would force him to stop. He would fling his arms around himself, hug himself tightly trying to keep his chest and vital organs warm, maybe jump up and down as his toes began to burn, then to ache, and then grow numb. That he had no coat—did he have a shirt on at least?—she could not quite imagine. All she knew for sure was that at forty below his nose and cheeks and fingers would be frozen in two or three minutes. And his shoulders. His back.

For a while he would cling to the hope that this was just a terrifying practical joke, a stunt designed to frighten him, that those who had abandoned him there would return for him, and he would be saved. But as the moments passed and the pain began to die away as his body slowly froze, he would know he was about to die.

Would he scream then to the animals hibernating in the

ground under the bush along the road? To the stars so cold and far away? To his Creator to help him? Soon, though, his frozen legs would no longer hold him upright and he would fall. Or maybe he would lie down quietly, curl into a ball, and wait for death to come to him.

They say at the end, finally, you just go to sleep, she thought. Slowly, as the night wore on, the warmth from his body meeting the freezing air would form a coating of frost on his body. How the crystal covering would sparkle in the starlight.

She put her face in her hands. Already she knew that the forces that run the world would not care about the deaths of two more aboriginal men, that in this too, there would be no justice, at least none worthy of the name.

Bonny woke in the night. Ross lay beside her on his stomach, his face turned away from her, one leg trailing over the side of the bed, the other bent at the knee, forcing her to the far edge of the mattress. She had thought she might soothe him with sex, but he had pushed her away angrily, as if the very idea sickened him, and she wondered, too disconsolate even to cry, where he thought he might find solace, if not with her, his wife, the mother of his children. He'd gone to sleep finally, well after midnight, and now he was snoring loudly while she lay rigid beside him. With so little room she couldn't even put her arms down by her sides, she got up, put on her dressing gown, and taking the tangled quilt from the floor where Ross had kicked it, went to the living room to sleep on the sofa.

For a long time she lay awake staring at the ceiling, shivering with the chill that had invaded the house, despite the quilt tucked tightly under her feet and pulled up under her chin. Ross wouldn't leave the farm until every last shred of hope had been dissolved. He would make their departure as long and painful as it could possibly be. Their marriage might even break up over it. She could foresee the long arguments into the night, Jason growing defiant and belligerent, Pammy silent and thin, her very thinness a steady threat.

The house was old, and the living-room window's seal had broken, leaking moisture at the bottom, and there was a diagonal crack across it. The moonlight had turned the crack into a meandering silver filament; along the window's bottom a crystal forest of frost ferns glittered. For some reason, Denise McKenzie came into her mind. She had thought the one good thing was that Denise didn't know that the women gossiped about her. But it seemed to her now that Denise did know—otherwise, she would have come to sit with them instead of standing alone on the far side of the rink, not even looking at them. How unhappy it must make her, Bonny thought, the women do it deliberately to make her unhappy, and she thought about the men at work who teased the retarded man until he cried, and about the women of Ross's family who did not, who never would welcome her into their family even though her children's blood was their blood. She thought of the bankers and investors who had never even seen the West, never met one of the people whose lives they were destroying, never would meet them. She thought of the aboriginal men frozen to death on a country road. Because they were troublesome, and they were only Indians.

It came to her then, as she lay there gazing at the way the moon filtered through the frosted glass, that all of these things belonged together, were part of the same thing. And what that thing was, it seemed to her now, as she lay alone shivering in the silence of the house, was a dark stain that spread everywhere, reaching to touch them all. She could see it: thick, black, and tar-like, oozing slowly, remorselessly. Some people built the simplest, homeliest dikes against it, holding it out, but most people were careless and its vileness touched them, here and there, every now and then. She could feel the sticky, black weight of it on all sides and she wanted to hold it off, but she wasn't sure she knew how. She wasn't sure she was strong enough.

In a while she heard Ross getting up and going into the bathroom and then the kitchen. She could tell he was trying to be quiet so as not to wake anyone, and finally she got up and in mutual, not-uncomfortable silence, cooked him breakfast, and sat with him as he ate it and talked softly to her about the things he needed her to do this week while he was in the city, and about the needs of the children—new boots, a book for school—and how they would pay for them.

As he was leaving, she went with him to the door and lifted her face to kiss him. He bent to meet her lips, even as his eyes avoided hers. She listened to the crunch of his boots crossing the frozen yard in the absolute stillness and darkness of the early morning, to the truck start, rumble for a while, and then roll away out of the yard. Because it was too early to wake the children for school, she went back to lie on the sofa, and soon drifted into a troubled sleep.

She was in a forest—she recognized it as the temperate rain forest of the West Coast where she had been once, as a child, on a family holiday. She walked on a carpet of needles, spongy and moist under her feet, the air was humid, filled with the scent of rain, and of the fir and spruce trees, and some other fragrance she couldn't identify. But these massive tree trunks with the shredding, reddish bark were cedars—it was cedar that she smelled.

The trees soared above her into darkness, and she saw that at all their bases ferns of every kind and size grew: some had fringe so delicate it looked as if green clouds had settled on their stems; some were wider and taller than she was, and on these she could see clearly the intricate symmetrical patterns of their edges as the fronds rose in widening bouquets from the damp, rusted earth. The ferns rustled, whispering softly to her as she passed.

After a while she came to a clearing in the centre of which stood a palm tree. She walked closer to it, and then she understood that it was not a palm tree at all: it was a fern tree. She had not known until now that there was such a thing as a fern tree and the discovery shocked and pleased her; its existence seemed to her grave and important, and she walked around it, gazing at it in wonder and enjoying its beauty.

She fell into a deeper, dreamless sleep. When she woke sometime later with a start, it was still dark, and the furnace was stirring the window drapes. She saw that the frost on the glass had begun to melt. In excitement, she thought, *It's a chinook!* and listened for its hollow roar. But the only sound was the whirr of the furnace and the soft brushing of the curtains against the wall. The warm air rising through the floor vent below the window was melting the frost.

Still, she felt better, as if there really were a chinook sweeping over the plains, eating the snow and ice, warming the frigid air. She saw the countryside green again, birds enlivening the sweet spring air, and green buds opening on the trees in farmyards. It would come eventually, if she could just hold out, not give in, nor give up. The fern tree came back into her mind's eye and she held it there, as she lay on the sofa waiting for the children to begin to stir.

Acknowledgements

Thanks to my now-retired agent, Jan Whitford, who stuck by me through all the vicissitudes of a writer's life, always encouraging me, and doing her formidable best for my work. Thanks, of course, to Phyllis Bruce, my editor and publisher, whose "eye" is unmatched in my experience, and who sees what I don't see. To Jackie Kaiser, my new agent, and, as always, to my husband, Peter, without whom there would be no books.